"These poems are the work of a hungry ghost, a gifted young man with a keen eye and silver tongue, who felt in the keenest, most intimate way the transience of all things. Jim Nawrocki alternates between a Buddhist calm and the ferocious appetite for the life of those condemned to know they will die young. In these splendid verses only Jim's art is resolute and invariably mature."
—**Edmund White**

"An unsung genius in life, Jim Nawrocki's poems and stories left me wanting much more and knowing my hunger wouldn't be satisfied. Alternating between the domestic, the postapocalyptic, and the cosmic, *House Fire* marks not only the beginning, but also the end, of Jim's vision. This ironic circularity perfectly encapsulates his erotics. If we are lucky, more posthumous work will grace us with his peculiar wisdom."
—**Michael Walsh, editor of *Queer Nature* and author of *Creep Love***

"Jim Nawrocki's tales draw the reader into their diverse worlds with a rare, almost startling immediacy. His clear vision and technical command take the everyday, and the arcane, and render them vivid, numinous—and unforgettable."
—**Ian Young, author of *London Skin & Bones: The Finsbury Park Stories***

"*House Fire* reveals the heat, light, and rigorous compassion of Jim Nawrocki's singular mind. This is a book to devour in a hungry rush of curiosity and then savor in unhurried re-readings for the rest of your life."
—**Hilary Holladay, author of *The Power of Adrienne Rich: A Biography***

"The poems of Jim Nawrocki – experiences of love, loss, memory and childhood – resonate with tenderness from the elegance and clarity of his talent and technique. They remain as luminous as celestial bodies in the dark of night."
—**Todd Swindell, editor of *I Am Going to Fly Through Glass: The Selected Poems of Harold Norse***

HOUSE FIRE

by

Jim Nawrocki

7.13 Books
Brooklyn

Printed in the United States of America

First Edition

Cover art by Gigi Little
Fiction edited by Leland Cheuk
Poetry edited by K.B. Thors

Library of Congress Cataloging-in-Publication Data

ISBN (paperback): 979-8-9853762-2-7
ISBN (eBook): 979-8-9853762-3-4
LCCN: 2022932850

INTRODUCTION
BY MICHAEL CARROLL

I WILL QUOTE WITH minimal explication Jim Nawrocki's mysterious and lengthy beauty "The Ballad of Tangleton," which is the quietly propulsive, tone-setting first short story of this collection of fiction and poetry.

> *Severin Park was, almost literally, a work of art. The creation and crowning achievement of Chansen Soo Park, the eccentric, reclusive, and infamous cybernetics genius of Seoul, Severin had been the world's first fully functioning automaton (to use the archaic parlance his creator preferred). He was virtually indistinguishable from a human, but for the strange and almost ethereal cast of his skin, which Park père had fashioned from a mysterious kind of ceramic, durable and specially developed for his robotics work.*

Early this morning, after an evening of carefully rereading "The Ballad of Tangleton," I woke up from a vivid dream about a town where moralistic mobs take care of local sinners with violent, desperate repentance. My dream was the cartoon or video-game version of what Jim is getting at in "The Ballad of Tangleton." His vision of a post-apocalyptic world, rendered at least in his cool, rational cyborg's point of view (a clever update of the typical and familiar sangfroid of traditional noir heroes, including those of Philip K. Dick), proceeds in chilled expositions.

*But all this had been before the plague and the Ring bombings and
the global devastation mankind had wrought, as well as the subsequent disintegration of most of the world's civil, economic, and social
structures. Severin was able to survive these dark ages and bide his
time . . .*

Jim would survive a year or so into our disastrous previous
presidential administration, already getting a full picture of the
man's complete dereliction of duty. But the mishandling of the
COVID-19 pandemic would not come until nearly two years after
Jim's death.

The fictional Tangleton Severin travels almost daily to unload
twentieth-century souvenirs (old banknotes, glossy magazines featur-
ing naked Asian boys) for the rich inhabitants who escaped the terrorists' global blast is somewhere in the vicinity of New Sydney. He goes
by train, noticing among the other passengers the "marks of the plague
and the associated events . . . even after all these years":

*. . . He saw a hare-lipped infant, a few adults with smallpox scars
and signs of the many other diseases that had either re-emerged, or
developed outright in the aftermath of all that had happened. . . .
this was, after all, a nation of mostly refugees now.*

Some have synthetic skin to cover the scars or fill in flesh burned
away from the fallout from the Ring bombings, effacing them almost
completely of expression. The luckier ones, he writes:

*…lived in well-guarded enclaves and were able to preserve a very
high standard of living; that prosperity seemed to be spreading, but
only a little. Some of them now were avid collectors of these increasingly rare remnants of twentieth-century urban life, particularly from
what had been the United States. Park, in his way, fed on this
strange commerce. His symbiotic relationship with Stroessner was of
a kind that made up a rather active, if select, specialty, and one that
provided easy access to an even more lucrative black market.*

The artifacts Stroessner deals in cater to a well-heeled gay crowd—S&M literature, postcards of George Platt Lynes reproductions. Severin Park is gay at a time when the future of gays in New Australia is uncertain. The narrator refers to the dealer's gaze of "persistent, sad hunger," and we don't yet know Stroessner is aware of the clandestine gay affair Park is having:

That evening, the dark-skinned young man had returned and was waiting for Park who, feeling optimistic after his exchange with Stroessner, nodded to him as a signal that he should follow him up. Park had not forgotten the young man's sweet smell, the almost desperate strength of his arms around him. They made love intensely, and then lay talking as the sounds of the late-week evening traffic came up to them through the closed window lattices.

"It's riskier, now, isn't it?" said Park. The young man—Park still didn't know his name —answered without hesitation. "It is. The traditionalists seem to have taken a harder line with this sort of thing. I've even heard of a few disappearances, here and there. But of course you never see anything in print."

The relationship gradually develops and the conversations become less reserved between him and the boy, whose name he ultimately learns is Tadeusz, and who has his ear to the ground, tells Severin, "Morality is becoming a more important issue."

Two pages later, the story ends.

"Brava, Cassiopeia" is an X-ray of grief, monochromatically radiant with loss and longing. In the story's earliest moments, Lauren learns of her fiancé Ronald's sudden collapse in a separate gallery of the museum they're visiting together. "Insensible," he dies of a massive coronary in the hospital. Lauren hasn't been permitted to say goodbye. It is a typically lonely moment in *House Fire*. There's not a soul in the pages of fiction making up the first half of this book who is not somehow profoundly alone, even if eventually loneliness is redeemed in one ecstatic revelation experienced in a character's solitude. If loneliness is not the collection's overall theme, solitude and the gathering of each protagonist's thoughts, as they progress into the future, simply *getting on*, are part of Nawrocki's mordantly realistic view of life:

> *Until one day, she had to close the door to [Ronald's friends] and just pick up, resume what life she could. And she tried. But she knew it would take time. A lot of time. Her therapist had assured her of that.*

Lauren finds strength in the loss-surveying exercise of meeting friends who have gone through similar loss. "Her grief was hers, but she was not alone." A girlfriend's fiancé dies in a flash, while exercising at the gym. "She'd never be the same, Lauren knew, just as she herself never would be. Still, there would be life again."

And life does go on. Lauren finishes graduate school and applies to and is accepted for a fellowship in Berlin, and there she meets Marvin, who quickly goes from being a friend to being a lover. "They'd had a decent interval of courtship. It was clear there was a future for them, and in due time, after nearly a year of dating, then living together, they were married." The language of domestic rotation and the gradual development of life's usual anticipation of events is flat and gray, but emotions glow through. In the margins and white spaces between printed words, few of us would be unable to provide our own whimpers, gasps, or nods of emotional recognition.

"There are no rules for grief," says Tim, a gay friend recoupled after the death of his previous lover from AIDS. "There's no guidebook."

The moment in the dark, cavernous restaurant dissipates, Lauren says goodbye to the men, and in what resolves ultimately in a typical Nawrockian fashion, she is caught in a memory that is rich in—and only later to be contemplated by us—symbolism. One initially superseded by this daring and baldly revelatory, if not quite sentimental, epiphanic curtain-closing setup:

"She remembered how, a week or so before she'd left for Berlin, she'd gone back to the museum. She'd needed to revisit the spot where Ronald had collapsed. She might as well say *died*. He'd been gone by the time they'd found him, his essence, his consciousness, in all likelihood, unavailable to her. Still, she'd whispered to him in the ambulance, hoping some semblance of him heard." (Gratefully, she finds the museum empty.) "She took a seat in front of the big canvas."

It is the one Ronald was looking at when he collapsed. "She wasn't sure what her reaction would be, but she felt she had to finally confront it."

Fittingly, the painting Ronald was studying (or else not) just then is a huge abstraction.

Lauren sits and contemplates writing the Australian artist, Judith Whiteman, a letter, but a letter about what? What happens next (abstractly, and purely mentally) is what I now call one of Jim's outburst resolutions, distant landmines: here, a sudden memory of the painting which sets up the denouement, just before the next act of her life is to begin. There is a flash of epiphany in the hypothetical missive's conclusion, and that's it—the story, "Brava, Cassiopeia," ends.

In "Cold Front," the older, chemo-debilitated Harlan limps toward his own personal denouement, aided by his much younger and more spirited and vital caregiver Brandon. He is caught constantly in memories: "He couldn't remember when he'd last felt the old fire, the drive, libido, horniness . . ." And then Brandon is hospitalized after a sudden and serious car accident, and lies in a coma. Harlan looks out the waiting room window over the San Francisco skyline:

> *. . . he could see the rooftop of a building that he realized was the home of a longtime neighborhood Italian restaurant, a place he'd frequented since he'd first moved to the area in the early 1970s. Why in God's name he should be thinking of all that now he had no idea. But somehow those memories of comfort and old friendships made him saddened all the more at this news about Brandon.*

Brandon dies, and while absorbing this Harlan has a dream about working at a tollbooth, where car after car advances through the gate, until one curious customer pulls up:

> *. . . It rolled dutifully to a stop, and the young man at the wheel turned to look at him, making no move to offer any money for the fare. In fact, he made no move at all. He simply stared at Harlan. It was his own, youthful self, the beautiful young man he'd once been.*

Jim Nawrocki died on May 31, 2018, of liver failure resulting from the metastized colon cancer he'd been diagnosed with three years earlier.

Reel back to 1992, twenty-six years before—when I first met Jim in his native Toledo, briefly, as we were each about to begin a journey away from the Midwest toward our mutually chosen literary futures. He looked the very image of one of the Bright Young Things, a Thirties group of ambitious London socialites that included Cecil Beaton, Harold Acton, Evelyn Waugh, Patrick Balfour, and John Betjeman, among the dozens. We were in a disco and Jim was tall and broad-shouldered, with artfully clipped and heroic, Oxbridge dirty-blond hair. Immediately in the middle of all that gothy, earnest and loud dance rhythm, I knew that I'd met a man who'd be with me in spirit for the long run, even though in a matter of days I was planning to return to my hometown in Florida. Jim predicted my regrets for my decision to go back—not on romantic grounds but because he thought that as a gay man I would artistically perish amid the swamps and scrub of the overheated, benighted Southeast. Though wedding bells were not in the offing, we began a letter correspondence that lasted all through our separate peregrinations. And then in 1995 we got together for the first time again in Chicago.

By then I was living in Paris. Jim came to my new partner's book tour reading. Much the saucier one from the start (that reads "codependent"), I'd written my literary hero, Edmund White, a fan letter from the Czech Republic (where I was finishing up a stint in the Peace Corps) to Ed's adoptive home of Paris. Now Ed and I were living and travelling together.

It is foolish and self-defeating to overlook the silver-screen truism that nothing succeeds like success. (Ed later left Paris for my sake and ultimately we would relocate to New York via Princeton—he'd accepted a job there to keep me happy—because, truly, no one in Europe cares about an unpublished American writer. But yes, contacts make a difference.)

Jim had already started publishing reviews and essays in The *Gay & Lesbian Review* and the *Bay Area Reporter* on queer subjects as broadly ranging as Pedro Almodóvar, Gus Van Sant, Yukio Mishima, Bayard Rustin, Jann Wenner, Harold Norse, Tom of Finland, Herbert Huncke, Disco, Derek Jarman, William S. Burroughs, and practically anything and everyone else adjacent to homosexuality. Ed admired Jim's quick, pithy takes on queer culture and would look up from the new issue of The *G&LR* and say, "You know, your friend Jim is so smart. How does someone that young get to be so smart?"

The evening in Chicago bears recounting. Ed was promoting a slender book about our neighborhood in Paris illustrated by his lover who had died the previous year. Ed's sister lives in Chicago, and we met her and Jim at the modestly attended reading, then went to dinner with them. Still smitten, I spent most of my time in the restaurant "catching up," which meant my constant beaming at Jim. This bothered the unjealous Ed not at all but distressed and insulted his sister. Years later, while Ed lay unconscious in a New Jersey hospital recovering from a massive heart attack and double-bypass surgery, I spent a few hours on my cell updating Margy. Finally she said, "You know, honey, when I met you way back when, here in Chicago, I'll admit I had my doubts." (Giggling.) "But then a couple of years ago, after Eddie had had his strokes and I was staying with you guys in your apartment, I remember one night we were having dinner and you brought something to the table, and you reached down and stroked Eddie's hair, just so tenderly. I thought that was wonderful."

Many years passed between Chicago and Jim's subsequent move to San Francisco. I only ever found myself on the West Coast when Ed was touring another title. Once, still that dumb, presumptuous southerner, I waited until we arrived in the Bay Area to surprise Jim at the last minute. He was busy. For a while he'd been unemployed after moving there, but suddenly he was overwhelmed with freelance work to float him in the famously overheated Silicon Valley economy. And then we lost touch, except in the sense of the curiously slippery way you crossed paths on Facebook—commenting on each other's posts, and saying little else that's personal.

And then, as things would have it, he messaged me on Facebook with the news that he was ill.

Could it be that after those first few days of our seeing each other in Ohio, I saw Jim only twice over the years before his death? First in Chicago, and then sometime in 2017 in New York when he and his husband and long-term partner were visiting, and we had lunch?

Already Jim was reduced and pale, whittled and chalky, but his undaunted sweetness did shine through.

Something minuscule has come asunder.
Void, that old insatiable giant, grows a little.
I have to walk down the hall because of a need.

What I want
is to draw back together what's been broken,
to let flow the curious water of repair.

I glow metastatic now, I'm a colander for light, blast me
with the rays of revelation and tell me what the shadows say,
the ones left behind, pulsing, rabid, and dirty.

Fuck them for staking a claim and refusing to go politely.
I told their kind as much after my father turned yellow
and shrank gradually into nothing but not before

he moaned from out of a morphine meander
and I spoke, trying to breach the thickness of his pain,

and knew he didn't hear his son . . .

I cut that last line off; this is the first half of "The Hex Shank." The son realizes, now that he is cancer-stricken and in treatment, the disconnect he shared with his own metastatic father earlier. The poems are both more autobiographical and cancer-concerned than the stories:

The beginning of "Bitter Melon Soup":

My Chinese mother-in-law
beckons us to suburbia
where we journey to receive

this thin yellowish-brew
that's steeped for days.
Good for cancer she tells me,

and then in Cantonese
to Jason, begins
to explain the process

of how to boil bones
and slice with precision
the oblong, warty melons,

to create the mix and
allow the proper time
for the blend to become

what it must . . .

The effect of the final product the voice describes as

like a breeze over a cemetery slope
bearing traces of wavering smoke
that rises from offerings for the dead.

In "Body Blow," Jim reads Whitman, creating a single chunky prose poem, a paragraph of lusty and resigned, romantic, weathery detail, shaken with emotional gust:

> *. . . I'm holding the phone in the main room, looking back now at Whitman left open in the kitchen, my doctor's voice on the other end, like it's farther away than this city — he says,* I don't have good news *— I think,* Not now *. . .*

Later:

> *. . . I imagine a time, in some bed in some room, when, like one of Whitman's young soldiers, caught within a failing body, I will look up and maybe see the old whitened father himself, the poet at my bedside, his face bright with the love of comrades . . .*

Jim can go deep into mythology and mine the figurative and ecclesiastical to create a new oracular sense of things, as in his poem about proto-Beat Herbert Huncke, "St. Huncke":

> *Christ was hung*
> *between two thieves*
> *and forgave them*
> *amid the blaze*
> *and fly buzz of Golgotha.*
>
> *Maybe he reckoned*
> *that thievery is nothing*
> *if not a borrowing of glory,*
> *a barter no worse*
> *than a small deception,*
> *and worthy of mercy.*

Jim's husband, Jason Wong, figures in a number of these poems including "Moby":

> *I met him online—fantasy matched for fantasy,*

and when I saw him for the first time, walking to me
down the hill from where he parked his storied wreck,
I stood in my gate thinking he's too young, but I stayed.

"Ellipse" begins with Jason returning with Jim to Jim's home in
Ohio:

My first neighborhood,
> *my solar system.*

I enter its far edge with you,
> *show you the market, now abandoned,*

the drugstore, defunct too,
> *these, the outer belt's dead ice.*

And tightens the cord as they move toward the house where Jim
grew up:

I see my two brothers, myself, again,
> > *we three, directed*

to pluck Autumn's fallen flames
> > *off of our lawn,*

my mother upstairs . . .
> > *. . . my father down,*

each of them
> > *at their window.*

And:

I've brought you here as my witness,
but now you show me the world.

I mourn the Jim I knew, movie-star handsome yet always laughing off the compliments. But more than that, I celebrate the talent who over time wrought these quietly mature treasures.

STORIES

THE BALLAD OF TANGLETON

SEVERIN PARK WAS, ALMOST literally, a work of art. The creation
and crowning achievement of Chansen Soo Park, the eccentric,
reclusive, and infamous cybernetics genius of Seoul, Severin had
been the world's first fully functioning automaton (to use the
archaic parlance his creator preferred). He was virtually indistin-
guishable from a human, but for the strange and almost ethereal
cast of his skin, which Park *père* had fashioned from a mysterious
kind of advanced ceramic, durable and specially developed for his
robotics work.

Severin had become a celebrity of sorts. He'd been deliber-
ately gifted with a combination of a face and physique considered
both unusual and attractive. Seen often at art and fashion-world
fetes, he had more or less stumbled into a kind of side career as
a model, appearing in several high-end European fashion magazines. He'd had some roles in films in what had been called independent cinema. He was even something of a playboy; his creator
had also taken care to endow Severin with not only the functioning anatomy required for physical intimacy, but the desire (albeit
a moderate one) to use it as well, and there hadn't been a shortage
of women, or even of men, who coveted the chance to earn a turn
in Park's bed.

His wealthy creator had appeared indifferent, at least publicly, to the unusual life assumed by his handiwork. His only formal statement on the matter had been a manifesto, which, true to his preference for old technologies, he published in a limited edition and expensively produced letterpress book, *On the Moral Autonomy of Automatae*. As its title suggested, one of its proposals was a radical addition to the system of Linnaean taxonomy, a recognition of cybernetic creations and artificial intelligences as worthy categories of "life." The manifesto was quickly reproduced on electronic media and available to everyone. It was widely read and debated at the time. While it was clear that the inventor had used his considerable wealth to finance Severin's emergence into the world at large, it was also evident that, after a certain interval, the quasi-human being he created had been able to support himself and live independently. Park and his creator had little contact after that threshold had been crossed.

But all this had been before the plague and the Ring bombings and the global devastation mankind had wrought, as well as the subsequent disintegration of most of the world's civil, economic, and social structures. Severin was able to survive these dark ages and bide his time, but he emerged in a new order within which he was unknown, his previous fame like something from a long-ago dream. For this, actually, he was ultimately thankful. Like so many others, he had waited and struggled, and had come through as the slow, modest, but steady efforts at reconstruction took hold and gathered momentum. The new world was clearly scathed, still reeling in many respects, but something that promised to endure had come through.

Park stood on the platform. The evening train from Tangleton to Vanderwort Station was unusually crowded, but he managed to find an empty seat. He was lucky, because it was a long ride back and an uncomfortable one if the air conditioning, a recently reinstated luxury, suffered one of its frequent breakdowns. He let his hands rest on his valise and ran through his mental list of what it contained, wondering if it were all as valuable as he'd hoped.

Or at least as interesting. *Remnants of the lost world*, Stroessner had once called the items of their trade. Park looked at random faces in the crowd, wondering what they remembered, or chose to remember, of the earlier times. Most sat quietly, their bodies strangely luminous in the light of the advancing sunset coming through the wide windows of the old passenger car.

The crowd. It was, Park thought, a sure sign that things had started to improve. New Australia Rail, now firmly established after its slow post-crisis-era beginning, was doing a good business, and there were more than a few people, like him, who were well dressed and healthy looking. Still, the marks of the plague and the associated events were apparent even after all these years. He saw a hare-lipped infant, a few adults with smallpox scars and signs of the many other diseases that had either re-emerged or developed outright, in the aftermath of all that had happened.

As if to reassure himself, Park cracked open his valise and tucked his hand inside. It was a familiar assortment: some old paperbacks and glossy magazines; a carefully wrapped bundle of rare paper currency, mostly deteriorated, unearthed not far from one of the relatively untouched sites in old Sydney and in the areas north of Tangleton. And there were the special finds as well. Park wasn't sure how much value Stroessner would place on them. He was a hard man to read, an experienced fellow well practiced in the art of negotiation. Still, Park had his ways of getting to him.

The train stopped at one of its checkpoints about halfway to New Sydney and more passengers boarded. A small buzz started to run through the car. Park heard murmurs in various languages; this was, after all, a nation of mostly refugees. He saw an Aboriginal woman look up from her newspaper and down the aisle before she quickly looked back to her reading, trying to conceal her agitation. He figured it was one of the regional government's police patrols, and he'd guessed right.

Stroessner, repository of history that he was, referred to the police as the Gestapo, and Park had learned to appreciate the dark joke. Initially, surviving portions of the country's army had organized to manage the consequences of the plague, the Ring bombings, and the subsequent riots, migrations, and civil breakdowns. Those first attempts at order gradually became an extended effort to rebuild and reorganize. In those years, the government, such as it had been, was forced to deal with the influx of plague and Ring bombing refugees. After people began to regroup in what was reclaimed or newly built in the cities, the government solidified its structure and broadened its mission, targeting prostitution and other so-called moral offenses. In recent years, their goals had become less clear, and they put everyone on edge.

The two uniformed men made their way down the aisle of the car without stopping. Perhaps they had other issues at hand. Park had nearly settled back into a kind of half-doze when a subtler, different kind of ripple disturbed the relative tranquility of the train ride. The Aboriginal woman looked up and quickly down again and when Park looked he saw them as well: two Ring Bomb survivors had entered at the last station and were finding their way to some seats. He heard the slow, telltale hiss of their breathing, a sound augmented by their respiratory implants.

They took their place in two of the seats that had cleared, almost diagonally in Park's line of sight. In the short interval after they'd settled in, he dared to look at them. Their injuries were typical of far-boundary survivors: the flat, almost featureless face and filmed over area of what was now eye membrane. Park thought of the folklore. In some places, they were still revered as seers. Was it surprising, this weird veneration? They frequently traveled in pairs or groups, and their gesture-based language and its rapid tactile exchanges always drew stares. Perhaps the effect was enhanced by the recent evidence that their numbers were dwindling. People assumed the survivors were simply dying out, but a few told tales of secret settlements and cults. Park saw others glancing, troubled by the same low-level unease that Ring victims always seemed to generate.

Just as Park was watching them he thought he saw one, then the other, move their faces in his direction. They seemed female, more in bearing than in physical characteristics. One had her fingers busily communicating along the exposed forearm of her companion. Park flushed in embarrassment, as if they could actually see him, and immediately looked away. He silently cursed his creator. *Human, all too human,* he thought. At times like this, he wished he'd been given the advantage of not having emotions. Instinctively, he reached up to adjust his tie, suddenly feeling guilty for the opulence of his clothes and his shoulder-length black hair. He thought of Stroessner and his upcoming transaction with him, eager to distract himself with the realities of his routine. Stroessner, he knew, liked Park's sartorial flair. It was all part of the very things that had given Park his edge with the old man. He turned to regard the sun-drenched landscape passing outside the train windows. There, at least, was something that seemed constant, still natural, untroubled. Out there, it had been like that for as long as anyone could remember.

The next day, Park made his way along Macquerrie Boulevard, passing the fronts of the broad neoclassical facades, remnants of the old city that had survived the fires. He found the alley and turned to enter the relatively dark arcade that housed, among others, Stroessner's shop. He was grateful for the shade, because the heat of New Sydney was at its worst this month.

The night before had been unsettling. Park, of course, didn't sleep . . . but he did enter a kind of dormancy. "Your quiescent state," Chansen had explained to him so long ago. "I've built it in so that you can live more like people do." "Will I dream?" Severin asked. "In a manner of speaking. Your . . . cognitive powers never really require rest, per se, but when you're dormant, they will assume a kind of cycle of their own. You might experience what we could call a mild hallucinatory state." For some reason the noise from the avenue below his apartment had distracted him. He'd been more worried than usual about the valise, but after locking its contents in the safe and pouring himself a bit of bourbon (a gift from one of the Tangleton merchants), he'd been able to relax only slightly. The young, dark-skinned man who sometimes worked in front of the building had had his eyes out for Park, and he'd almost changed Park's mind, but at the last minute Park demurred. He found it astonishing, still, that the young man had been able to speak passably good Korean and had managed to surmise it was Park's native language, and this surprise, more than anything else really, had prompted Park to let him come to his room those first few nights. Surprise and, he had to admit, the sheer risk of it. But the young man was handsome, and seemed drawn to Park for similar reasons, so much so that, after two or three visits, he had stopped hinting to Park about payment, and even refused it when Park insisted. Last night, though, Park didn't want the risk of such solace. Not until he'd looked down from his window to see the youth amble slowly from view did he think about sleep.

Midway down the arcade Park entered the elaborate door under the simple sign—ANTIQUITIES—above Stroessner's shop. It hadn't been there all that long, in the grand scheme of things, and was one of the many manifestations of New Sydney's gradual turn to prosperity. Stroessner, Park knew, could remember a lot worse, more so than Park. The old German had been among those prescient enough to profit from the small but elite wealthy class that had managed to emerge in the wake of the plague and the crises. They had known enough to prepare, to flee the cities, and to consolidate their resources for the eventual reemergence of order. Or at least a kind of order. They lived in well-guarded enclaves and were able to preserve a very high standard of living; that prosperity seemed to be spreading, but only a little. Some of them were now avid collectors of those increasingly rare remnants of twentieth-century urban life, particularly from what had been the United States. Park, in his way, fed on this strange commerce. His symbiotic relationship with Stroessner was of a kind that made up a rather active, if select, specialty, and one that provided easy access to an even more lucrative black market. As Park came through the door he smelled the shop's comforting, stale aroma, a mixture of old paper and tobacco smoke.

"Ah, Mr. Park," Stroessner called out in his faint European accent. "What do we have today? Perhaps some mid-twentieth-century samizdat? Sheet music from the nineteen thirties?" His tone was playful. "I don't suppose you've come to fulfill an old man's dreams, eh?"

Stroessner seemed strangely jubilant. Park hadn't seen him as cheerful since the antiquarian had shown him that cache of Thai magazines, the young men with smooth, lightly muscled bodies, the images spread across nearly singe-free glossy pages, bright Thai letters and Chinese characters emblazoned on their covers. It had been one of his early attempts to read Park. Park knew it was the rarity of such publications, more than their salacious content, which truly delighted Stroessner.

"Come back," said Stroessner, waving Park through the little wooden gate that led to his office. It was here that the old man kept the long display table, the lights and the magnifiers he used for his work. "Let's see what you have."

While Stroessner checked an ancient coffee brewer and poured a cup for himself, and tea for his visitor, Park carefully unpacked the contents of his valise. He arranged the old paperbacks and magazines off to the side, and Stroessner, moving closer, regarded them with only mild curiosity. He grew more interested as Park removed and placed an enigmatic brown bundle, slightly smaller than the dimensions of a paperback, near the center of the open table space.

Park smiled at Stroessner and took the tea he offered. "Something I knew would surprise you," he said as Stroessner, familiar with their rituals from long rehearsal, switched on a desk lamp and carefully unwrapped the parcel. As he did so Park noticed again the peculiar light of the synthetic skin that covered Stroessner's left temple and cheek, the odd purplish color always more visible in the direct light, a reminder of his exposure to Ring fallout.

As Park watched, he pulled out the bundle of glossy white cards emblazoned with large, thick black letters, BNE. Stroessner let out a sigh of satisfaction, quickly moving through the pack of identical decals, checking the quality of each one.

"A rare find indeed," he said, not hiding his excitement. "And the provenance?"

"You know how it is in Tangleton," said Park. "One can never be entirely sure, but I have it on relatively good faith that these were found in old Sydney. They were already a part of a collection, an old graffiti gallery."

"He never marked them, did he?" said Stroessner rhetorically, musing about the identity and methods of the now legendary early twenty-first-century graffiti-sticker artist. "Back in the old life, I saw one of these still intact on a concrete slab in Berlin. I think it had come from the San Francisco Bay Area. I could do a moisture analysis of these. That might tell us something."

"But it would probably be compromised, contaminated, don't you think?"

"Considering where it might have been? Yes," said Stroessner, carefully switching off the lamp. "But if any of these were Bay Area, that would mean they were acquired long before the Subduction Event."

Park tried to recall the date of that particular seismic disaster. It had been sometime around 2035, a few years before the Ring attacks and the start of the plague.

"But whatever the case, Mr. Park, you've uncovered a find. I'll draw you up a check right away."

Park gave him an inquisitive look, nodding toward the other items, the assorted books and magazines.

"Yes," said Stroessner. "Considering their overall quality, I'll take those too. They seem to move fairly well these days. Excellent work, Mr. Park."

Park was relieved that Stroessner was so amenable. He sat contentedly as the old man pattered on and busied himself with ledgers and paperwork.

"It amazes me that these things still manage to come through," said Stroessner. "The graffiti slabs are rare enough, and that's where the real money is, as you know. But Zilkowski has the market on those. If I were younger, maybe I could deal in them too."

He picked up the BNE stickers again. "But for these," he said, "it's astounding how many of the North American artifacts of such quality are still in circulation. You know they've started to make transports to the Far West again?"

Park was surprised. He'd heard rumors of isolated air transports, but news from North America was rare, and this particular piece had not yet reached Tangleton or any of the other trade bazaars. He guessed it would soon. Stroessner was usually true to his word, a good source of information. He was glad the old man trusted him enough to share it.

"Who would have thought?" said Stroessner, eager for the chance to discuss crisis history, a topic he could never resist. "The plague. The Ring bombs. It's almost as if the terrorists were responsible for both. Some still think they were."

Park watched curiously as Stroessner continued. "There used to be people, small dedicated bands, who dreamed of destruction like that. The Baader-Meinhof Group. The Middle East terrorists and of course ISIS," he said. Park watched Stroessner pause, as if trying to recall something.

"*A violent order, is disorder,*" Stroessner intoned, pleased with himself. He looked at Park pointedly. "That's Wallace Stevens. An American poet. Perhaps the reference is lost on you, Mr. Park? Leftists. Luddites. Anti-capitalists, in the end. They just wanted to take apart what seemed to be destroying us. Maybe they were right. To think they were able to pull all that off. It makes one consider those old ideas about God and punishment."

"Those old ideas might not be so dead after all," said Park.

They'd talked about it often enough. Park had noticed that men and women of Stroessner's generation, the very few he'd met, had an inherent need to meditate on crisis history. Park found Stroessner's discussions illuminating, and despite the vague unease engendered by the old man's thinly veiled attraction to him, he enjoyed his company.

Stroessner held out the check, written in his florid script, and Park placed it carefully in the inside pocket of his valise. The Bank of New Sydney had proven itself trustworthy, so Park felt he had little reason to worry. When he looked up, Stroessner presented him with a small parcel, not unlike the packet of BNE stickers that Park had just sold him.

"A small loan," said Stroessner. "Returning the favor, I suppose. I believe you will find this very interesting." Park occasionally got these gifts from Stroessner, and he wondered what it might be this time, some S&M literature? Postcards of George Platt Lynes reproductions? Park put the package quickly in his case, suddenly unsteady under Stroessner's gaze, nervous that the man's persistent, sad hunger might become overt.

That evening, the dark-skinned young man had returned and was waiting for Park who, feeling optimistic after his exchange with Stroessner, nodded to him as a signal that he should follow him up. Park had not forgotten the young man's sweet smell, the almost desperate strength of his arms around him. They made love intensely, and then lay talking as the sounds of the late-week evening traffic came up to them through the closed window lattices.

"It's riskier, now, isn't it?" said Park. The young man—Park still didn't know his name—answered without hesitation. "It is. The traditionalists seem to have taken a harder line about this sort of thing. I've even heard of a few disappearances, here and there. But of course you never see anything in print."

Park ran his hand over the young man's ridged abdomen, down his powerful thigh. He couldn't remember the last time he'd actually read one of the district newspapers. He heard the young man sigh beside him.

"A good time to be careful, I guess," said Park, by way of warning. He knew the young man had sense, the survivor's instinct. What Park wasn't certain of was whether this comforted him, whether he needed to reassure himself of it. Because what, after all, did this youth mean to him? They'd been careful, and yet they shared something that, unique in Park's experience at least, had been significant, a connection more than physical, more than the occasional, professional favors he'd enjoyed in Tangleton's alleys, for example, the ministration's of the young women sometimes foisted upon him by grateful merchants, a commerce that was as necessary for Park as it was uncomfortable.

"Are *you*?" he asked Park, ". . . careful? I would guess that whatever it is you do requires it. It seems like a safe assumption for just about everyone, around here."

"It is," said Park. "So what was it like for you, early on?"

The young man looked away, hesitant, silent. "Later," he finally said to Park, getting up to dress. "We can talk later, the next time."

It was as much of a promise as Park had had from anyone lately. Even his long business relationship with Stroessner was built upon a series of more tentative agreements, the sort of shared understanding that new arrangements might have to be made on relatively short notice. Park found himself ready to believe that there was more to the youth than he had originally surmised. He could, in fact, even look forward to a next time, if they were lucky enough to have one. He thought of him as a boy, almost, because he did look young, but he was likely in his early twenties, perhaps not more than ten years younger than Park himself. He'd been a lucky one, too, it seemed. His body looked to be unscathed by the diseases that had touched so many others.

After he left, Park remembered what Stroessner had given him. He retrieved it from his valise and returned to his bed with it. Underneath the brown wrapper, within a translucent, plastic preservative pouch, Park found a thick green book. It looked old, and had been bound with blank, unlined pages, which were written upon in a variety of inks. Sections had fallen out and others had been sewn in. Most of the pages were stained and dirty. Park began to read.

It's hard to believe it's just been a week. A week since Steven and I made it out of the city. A week since we fled with all the others. How could it all have changed so quickly? And it's just as hard to believe what we've heard. There have been so many rumors from people: That Sydney actually got off easy. That the Americans were the hardest hit. Some said it was decades in the making. So the fires we saw from far off were repeated just about all over the world. Who knows where we'll get to or what we'll do when we get there. Steven said our chances would be better if we stuck with one of the smaller groups.

A survivor's diary. Park had heard about them. They were rare. So why had Stroessner given him this one? Park paused and looked beyond the somewhat weak, dim circle of the lamp next to his bed to the different light coming up to his dark room from the street below. He guessed that the diary's author had been part of a group already making its way out of the city to escape the plague risk when the Ring events began. There had been a lot of people on the move in those days. There was a break of sorts, and the handwriting seemed to get clearer, easier to read:

I don't know how long it's been since I've had time to write. We're lucky. We heard from a group that met ours yesterday that whoever stayed in what was left of the cities had to contend with unspeakable brutalities.

There's talk of setting up a small settlement once we find someplace reasonably close to water. Davis told us that it's probably not too far north of here.

Another break, and then:

I told myself that I wanted a record of this, but there's much I don't want to remember. And too much of it is the same. Apparently some of those from one of the last planes that got here from Europe have been supplying a lot of information about what happened. We've heard more about what went on in the cities, and about all the ones who didn't get out in time. It didn't take long for tribes to form, for new reasons to fight. They all hate the past now. They burned museums. They burned libraries. Even in Sydney and Melbourne. In some cities the entire financial districts went up in flames. Sometimes I wonder how we did live like we did, how we ever allowed ourselves to think that it would never end.

Park thought of the young man and what he'd said, and he wondered if he'd hear the rest of his story. He tried to read more from the green book, but drowsiness soon overtook him, and he fell asleep.

In the weeks that followed, Park went about his usual business routine, riding the train out to Tangleton at least once or twice to see if his contacts had new material, to inquire among his network of connections and informers. He'd asked around, casually, for word of other existing settlements in the territory. This usually elicited curious, diplomatic smiles and, of course, a current of suspicion. Park had to be careful to not reveal too much, to drop just the right amount of hinting and hopefully elicit a careless revelation, perhaps over glasses of some locally made alcohol. But no mention of other settlements beyond the trade towns Park already knew about. Park had been sure to keep the green book locked away in his apartment safe. He had an instinct that Stroessner had entrusted it to him, and that there was a subversive quality, some kind of coded secret, in the book itself. The paucity of stories about other, previously unknown settlements confirmed that.

He hadn't seen the boy in several days, so he had time to read more. The diary's remaining installments were arranged in short, irregularly timed sections that the writer had eventually started to divide with an improvised calendar that seemed to mark its beginning from the time around the Ring events. From various clues in the diary, Park guessed that the writer was a relatively young woman, either the wife or partner of Steven. The other names mentioned, such as Davis, emerged in the chronicle as group leaders.

Day 112: Davis and the others think most of the building will be complete in another year, about the time they think that the weather patterns will start to normalize. Even though the bombs and the city fires put out a lot of debris, apparently it wasn't extensive enough for a full nuclear-winter scenario. But it's hard to say, given the way we've been getting information. Despite all the deliberate burning done for plague control, we've managed to scavenge a lot, but none of the radios we found worked. It's funny how we went back to those, hoping for something, after all this.

Day 170: Word has been getting out about us. We've had more additions in the last couple of months, and more news. A fundamentalist sect has built up one of the larger towns, about fifty kilometers west of us, and they've been preaching about the corruption of the secularists and the sodomites. Well, it proved to be pretty good advertising, from what we've been told. Steven thinks it's reason enough to establish some defenses, and he's probably right about that. Davis seems to agree. They're going to take it up at the next group meeting.

Year 2: Day 41: Last week Davis and some of the scouts and hunters came upon some wanderers a few miles out. Davis was suspicious at first, but then he saw that they were young . . . maybe twelve or thirteen years old at the oldest. He gave them some water and the kids told them that there's a lot of rebuilding going on, and that some of the cities are starting to repopulate the salvageable sections. Davis would have been inclined to disbelieve them but one of them had a crudely printed newspaper she said she'd picked up from a trade town, a kind of emerging barter economy that's spawned some elaborate settlement activity. The paper actually had announcements about the newly organizing regional governments and repopulation efforts. Davis is wary of it. When he brought the news back there was talk about leaving, about going back. Steven wants to stay.

The voice of the diary's narrator came to haunt Park. As he made his rounds between New Sydney and Tangleton, as he passed near the environs of Tangleton's Ring survivor encampment, or saw those with more prosaic scars who moved along Tangleton's crooked streets, he returned in his mind to the diary's writer and her compelling story. It was actually a dense chronicle, and Park had to take time to work through the often-unfamiliar vocabulary of its pages. The account read like a kind of intentional history for the group, a manifesto of separation. From clues in the narrative Park surmised that the group grew over time, but it also seemed to become more protective and selective.

Year 2: Day 75: A visitor. He calls himself McClarren. He told us more about what had happened in the cities, even in America and Europe. The riots. The massive book burnings. It confirms just about everything we've heard before. I guess it's not surprising that people have gone to religion in a militant way. They've been blaming godlessness for what happened and yet resorting to god-awful violence in the name of God. They used to talk about "the culture wars" and now it's happened, according to McClarren, in a very real way. The fundamentalists are trying to set up new governments in some of the cities, or they're starting new towns. They say they want to avoid the old mistakes. I suppose that's what we want too.

Year 2: Day 81: McClarren told us about the all-female settlements that have been talked about in the region. He saw at least one of them, he said, but he wasn't allowed to get too close. They were populous, and well armed. Steven laughed when he told me about it later. He thought it was too much like every man's fantasy. He was suspicious of McClarren at first, and he didn't want to give up too much information about us, but it eventually became clear that the old man didn't care, and that he wouldn't be staying on with us at any rate. Steven and the others figure he's just trying to get information from us before he moves on, trying to figure out if we have any agendas of our own. Davis now thinks of him as a kind of ally. McClarren gave us what information he could, and he even drew a fairly extensive map of the pattern of the settlements and townships farther out. If his information is at all reliable, and Davis has a hunch it is, we should be fairly secure where we are. Davis wants to keep building. McClarren promised to spread the word to the right people, and the wrong word to the wrong ones. We can only hope he's a man we can trust.

Park had at first wondered how much Stroessner had read of the green book, but now he was sure that he'd not only read it, but that he likely had more information about its origins. He might have even had a connection, through some chain of association, to someone from the actual settlement. As he was nearing the end of the chronicle, Park was hungry for clues to its location, and its fate. The writer seemed to have taken an approach, in the later pages, of deliberate vagueness. Park noticed, for example, how she eventually abandoned her system of dating the entries. The entries themselves became less frequent, then ended abruptly.

When he returned to Stroessner's shop, Park quickly steered the conversation to the topic of the diary. They had just finished another transaction. Stroessner handed Park his payment and sat back from the table and the ledger he just updated.

Park watched him raise his ancient hand and run it along the divide where Stroessner's synthetic skin met the real skin on the left side of his face.

"Fascinating, aren't they?" said Stroessner. "I come across them now and then, the diaries, the journals. I used to think they might be worth something, that people might take an interest in that part of our history. But it hasn't happened yet. I suppose when it does, we're all in trouble."

"Why do you say that?"

"When people want to tell and retell history, it just means that they want to control it."

"Whatever happened to just knowing it?"

"That's what I thought you wanted," said Stroessner, looking intently at Park. "That's why I gave you the book. Your parents must have been alive then." He paused, pointedly, then added, "Perhaps like your young friend's."

Park was momentarily startled that Stroessner knew about his lover, but the more he thought about it, the more it made sense that the old man had established ways of checking up on his contacts. Provenance. Wasn't that one of his watchwords? It could apply to people as well as things. He was pleased that Stroessner seemed to know nothing of his true identity, and was assuming a biological "provenance" for Park.

"A man like me," Stroessner said, "has to be careful. Please don't take offense, my friend."

What most bothered Park was not the spying, but the attempt to inquire about his origins. He preferred the uncertainty. So he'd let Stroessner think that he, like so many others, had once been part of a refugee family. In a sense it was true. He could let it go at that. Stroessner had his own reasons for trying to get closer to Park; Park still thought it best to keep him at bay.

"We can talk more the next time," said Park, leaving Stroessner's shop. He noted the older man's smile, unsure if it was fatherly benevolence or something else. He preferred to think it was the former.

Coming back from Tangleton on an evening train later that week, Park had found himself on one of the route's last runs, the car nearly empty. He'd just seated himself when he realized two Ring survivors sat at the far end of the car, facing him. He was uneasy at first, but this gave way to something even vaguer, and soon he was actually relaxed, allowing himself to be lulled into semi-drowsiness by the train's soothing motion. He allowed his dormancy to settle over him. He could just as easily have not done so, but he thought it wise to do so in public, so as to perpetuate the illusion of appearing as human. Bits of the day played across his mind, half-formed dreams, images and snatches of phrases from the merchants he'd visited earlier in the day.

"*Tangleton, Tangleton, that Tangle of a Town.*" He had stopped, earlier, to watch raucous street musician battering away on a reconstructed piano at a busy corner of Tangleton's dusty main intersection. It was a lively rendition of "The Ballad of Tangleton," a long historical chronicle, the lyrics of which were populated by a lively array of real and semi-folkloric figures who engaged in several dangerous and bawdy adventures. Park had laughed along with the crowd at the song's many jokes, and at the bantering shtick the performer had perfected with a huge cutout face of a woman from an old public transport advert. The crowd was loud with appreciative hoots and cheers.

The music played through Park's half-sleep, haunting now.

Something else intruded. Sounds, at first, then words. Unfamiliar, incantatory, like bits of poetry. *Bandicoot.* One said.

Baiame. Sky road.

Park felt his head jolt, as if shaken. When he rose back into full alertness, the train neared its approach to Vanderwort Station. He got up, almost groggily, to stand at the exit door closest to him. As the train slowed and he got ready to exit, he looked at the other end of the car, where the two Ring survivors stood waiting, still facing him. The door slid loudly open, but Park was hardly cognizant of it or of the steady traffic of people on the outside platform. Something new passed into his awareness. A voice, just behind him, said, "*This is the dreaming.*"

Back at Stroessner's shop a day later, Park related his strange experience on the train.

"The dreaming," said Stroessner, as if tossing the phrase like a ball, playing with its dimensions. "That's 'The Dreamtime,' the old mythology of this country. That much I can tell you. We haven't forgotten *that*."

"And those other words," said Park, confident that Stroessner, of all people, would know, "were place names?"

"Deities, more than likely," said Stroessner. "Gods. Spirits. The aborigines were a totemic people. The land and the sky were, to them, always alive with the spirit world, the creative power of time, what they called 'Dreamtime' or 'The Dreaming.'"

"But these were Ring survivors I saw," said Park, puzzling over it.

"Very likely aboriginal ones," said Stroessner. "Quite a few of them were in places where they got enough Ring fallout to change them, but not kill them."

The two were silent for a while, Park processing this information from Stroessner. "Maybe it's true what they say about them," said Park, "the telepathy and all that."

Stroessner looked at him, smiling lightly. "Well, it would help to be able to translate what you'd heard, but so many of those records, the anthropological fieldwork, the artifact collections . . . you know as well as I do, how most were destroyed in the crisis riots."

Stroessner regarded Park, intent on easing the younger man's mind. "You wouldn't be the first," he said. "Those Ring folk have a way of inducing this kind of response. Whether it's old-school trickery, or something else, I'm not so sure. But I rather like their invocation of the native gods."

Park thought it over. Stroessner lit one of his cigars, and the smoke soon settled into a gray-blue haze around the shop. Park let his eyes wander over the shelves and glass cases all around them. On the walls not taken up by shelves, Stroessner displayed framed prints, posters, and colorful old advertisements. Park tried to imagine what kind of world it had been when resources had been plentiful and there were whole industries devoted to selling things.

Park remembered the diary and their earlier conversations. "Do you ever regret coming back to the city? I still hear stories about other settlements, places off the map, better than Tangleton, maybe even better than this."

"Been thinking about the diary, eh?" Stroessner said, punctuating his rhetorical question with a long exhalation of smoke. "I suppose it's natural. I've heard the stories too, especially these days, with the government trying to come down a little harder."

"So you don't really know much about these people or even if they are, in fact, still there?" asked Park.

Stroessner shook his head and looked at him with what the younger man took to be an almost profound sadness.

"It came to me from someone I met while I was still moving through the settlements, before I figured it was safe to return to what they were making out of New Sydney," said Stroessner. "I didn't know much about him, only that he was dying, and that he seemed to trust me. But I tried to find them. Believe me, I did." Park studied the old man as he listened, imagining him as he'd looked when he was younger. Stroessner had a grave expression now, no doubt remembering willfully forgotten details about those difficult years.

"But if they are still there," said Stroessner, "well, I would hope that it's something that we can dream of." As Park got up to leave, Stroessner tapped the valise, where Park had placed the new check. "You might want to cash those soon," he said.

Park remembered the words from the boy, the hint that the traditionalist elements of the New Sydney government, as well as those of other regions, were asserting more authority. He wasn't sure how closely Stroessner was monitoring the situation, but he guessed that the old man had his ways. He had, after all, something of a reputation. Park had heard rumors that Stroessner managed to procure young men. But with Park and Stroessner, what they had in common had never been openly discussed. It had always been an undercurrent, a subtext. It was now merging closer to an openness that unsettled him. Park was not sure how much he could or how much he wanted to share with Stroessner. The book was an entreaty of sorts or at least an offering.

A few nights later, Park's lover returned. The young man followed him into the building carefully, at a distance, and even when sitting in one of the chairs in Park's front room, he seemed uneasy. The street was quiet that night.

Park, somehow sensing that he had to make the first move, stood up from his own chair and walked to the young man, standing over him, then reaching to caress his cheek.

"You owe me a story," he said, kneeling on the floor next to the chair.

The boy looked at him. "I could tell you anything," he said to Park. "And you wouldn't know the difference."

"I might," he said. "After all, each one of us has heard versions of it before. You were born somewhere out in the settlements or on your way there. They told you all about how the cities used to be, before everything happened. How it had been in Sydney, maybe. Or some of the others."

"They'd lived in Paris," said the young man. "And when things started to happen, they thought it might be safer here."

"How soon before they saw it coming?" asked Park. "Most people didn't."

"You're right," he said. "They were privileged. My father was a high-level minister in the Polish government. He'd been serving as a diplomat, first in Korea. Then Egypt. He met my mother in Cairo. They'd been in Paris and had heard talk within the intelligence circles about the new weapons, about how the terrorist coalitions were starting to organize and target the financial centers. Then the plague started. They were able to get to Sydney about a year before things really started to turn."

"History is hard to come by, these days," said Park.

"History is us, now," said the young man. "We're the ones who will have to make it."

"I still don't know your name," he said.

Park heard him say, "Tah-dosh."

"From your mother?" Park asked.

"My father, actually," said Tadeusz. "It's Polish."

He stroked Park's cheek. Park flinched instinctively, one more consequence of his creator's prescient and valuable attention to detail.

"The famous Severin Park," he said.

"So you know?" said Park.

"Of course. In the circles that my parents traveled in, your name came up a lot. And then I'd seen some of the pictures. Actually, I guess it's possible you met my parents or at least were in the same room with them . . ."

Park took Tadeusz's hand and kissed it. Then he stood, gently pulling the young man out of the chair. There was a hunger in his dark eyes that matched Park's. Tadeusz kissed him and soon they lost themselves in each other.

Somewhere in what seemed like a long course of his quiescent languor, Park saw images and experienced bits of random auditory stimuli in a way he never had before. "*Bandicoot*," a voice said. Park knew he recognized it, and the word.

"Who are you?" he asked. He stood in the open, sunlit outback with the sound of men and women chanting.

Baiame. Sky Father.

He saw a pair of hands, brown, old, caked with mud, smearing something ochre upon a small wooden carving.

All around him, the sky went from blue to deep crimson and then night, in a matter of what felt like moments. He saw the sky, star filled, like he'd never seen it before.

Park thought, but did not speak, "What is it I should do?" He looked again at the night sky, impossibly full of stars.

The voice said, *Find the water place.*

In the morning Park woke alone, the scent of Tadeusz still on his skin. He lay in bed for a few minutes remembering Tadeusz's departure in the middle of the night. He'd said something to Park that, heard in half sleep, Park could remember only vaguely, something about meeting up again soon.

Park wanted to believe he'd see his lover again, but things started to change dramatically in the next couple of weeks. The police units increased their activities in New Sydney and on the rail lines and in the towns and settlements that the lines connected to. Even in Tangleton, outside of the law as it had always been, the townspeople seemed to be clouded over with trepidation. Almost overnight, many of the merchants that Park dealt with regularly were under cover now. Park walked the normally crowded bazaar and it was quiet, and in the residential areas, all he could see as he passed along the narrow, meandering lanes were people going about domestic chores. A few of the food shacks were open, as usual, but their proprietors regarded him with something bordering on menace. Most of the visible signs of commerce, usually so prominent there, were hidden away, if not missing altogether.

Park was dismayed; if something momentous was coming, or indeed if it had already come, he hadn't heard anything about it from his networks, and the silence, this gulf of ignorance, did not bode well for his future.

If there had been any doubt in Park's mind about the tenor of these recent developments, it was settled toward the end of the week when he set out for Stroessner's shop and found it closed. When he approached the old arcade, he noticed the numerous uniformed patrolmen and the big trucks, something he hadn't seen much of in the city before. From the safe vantage of a vacant storefront nearby, a place with a concealed entrance that Park had known of, he watched the activity down toward the middle of the arcade. The police loaded boxes from Stroessner's shop into waiting trucks. Park felt the panic rise in him. It wouldn't be long before they found Stroessner's account books and worked out the identity of his suppliers, and Park would surely be one of their next targets.

Park hailed a rickshaw to speed back to his apartment, and he found that his door had already been opened. Panic nearly took him over again before he spotted Tadeusz sitting in his front room, looking resolute.

"I tried to catch you before you got to the arcade," he said as Park caught his breath and tried to calm himself. "It's been happening more. They're trying to do it quietly, but they're rounding people up."

"And doing what with them?" Park asked.

"Who knows? Morality is becoming a more important issue."

Park looked past Tadeusz and through the windows to the street below. So far, the traffic looked normal. "Do you think we might still have time to get out?"

"We have to leave today," said Tadeusz. "Do you have things you need to take with you?"

Park thought of the safe. He could empty it out; there wasn't much in it, except for the diary and some old coins, and he could leave his suits behind. Tadeusz had a bag of his own.

Park shed his business clothes and replaced them with dungarees and a pullover shirt. He had a tough old leather sack that he filled with the rest of what he needed, and after he emptied the safe, he spun the lock and shut the door.

"I have this for you," Tadeusz said.

Tadeusz held out a long envelope made of high-quality paper. Before Tadeusz said anything else, Park saw Stroessner's bold script on the front of the envelope where he'd written Park's name with his characteristic flourish. Silently, he took it from Tadeusz, stepping alone into the other room to read it. Stroessner's writing was as courtly as his speech:

Mr. Park,

You know, by now, that it's "falling apart" as they say. I suppose I figured I'd be in danger if it came to this, and I wasn't the only one to see the portents. Tadeusz and I have been in contact before, indirectly, I can assure you, but I've taken the liberty to use him as a kind of courier. I hope you won't mind.

I can only say this: you know that there are places for us. You've read the diary. If I manage to elude the government, I'm going to do my best to get there. I hope to see you again soon. Pardon the old expression, but Godspeed, Mr. Park.

W.S.

Walking into his kitchen, Park replaced the letter in its envelope and then struck a big wooden match and held it under a corner, letting the flame climb up the paper quickly and then dropping the blackening curls of it into his sink. He and Tadeusz watched it burn.

"You know about the place in the diary?" Park asked.

"I've heard talk of it. They're flourishing now, much bigger. It's a kind of paradise, if you know the way."

"Do you?"

"We start with Tangleton. If we move carefully, we can get to the right people," Tadeusz said. "And from there, it's about two or three days."

"I have what I need," said Park, leading Tadeusz out the door. In the street, the early afternoon traffic was getting busier, but still it betrayed few of the changes that were taking place all over the city. Park wondered if they would ever actually get to this place.

Too much could happen along the way, but he had to try, and he had to trust Tadeusz more than he'd trusted anyone. He fell into step beside the young man and together they walked purposefully, entering the stream of those making their way to the main station, and were soon lost in the crowd.

BRAVA, CASSIOPEIA

Something made Lauren look up from her phone, which she'd been using to take pictures. Something was happening where and when it should not have been happening. A man running. A large man, the weight of his urgency shaking the floor and causing a flutter among the quiet, ambling museum crowd. They now reminded her of startled birds, suddenly stirring from their stillness because of a potential predator.

What was this?

The man running was the tall Nigerian security guard from one of the galleries she'd passed through earlier. At least she'd guessed he was Nigerian. He'd reminded her of the men she'd seen working as barkers outside the arcades in Tokyo a couple of years ago. She had a vague memory of a Tokyo friend telling her that many men from that country seemed to gravitate toward those jobs. It was one of the quirks of the Japanese metropolis, its stunning grandeur and sheer audacity, that had surprised and amazed her.

She'd grown used to certain habits of travel, and even here, in her home city, she sometimes felt like a tourist, as she did now. Museums often made her sleepy, somnolent from the warmth of the crowds, the imperatives of having to look at and note the masterworks hung on the walls, each demanding attention, concentration, and time. She loved art, and considered herself open to the beauties offered by the painters and sculptors of just about every place and period. She was a scientist—an oceanographer—and because she spent so much time with data, and numbers, she'd always felt especially nurtured and restored by the varied beauties and pleasures of the visual arts. They required no quantification or calculation from her—she could simply *be* with them, and allow their majesty to settle upon her.

On this particular visit, with her fiancé Ronald, she'd been roving alone among the Abstract Expressionists—Pollock, Kline, and Rothko were her favorites, especially Rothko. She loved getting lost among them; there was something aquatic about many of their canvases, all that deep, silent drifting, or those occasional bursts of arresting color. It was when she was admiring a de Kooning that she happened to glance around the room and was taken with the handsome, powerful-looking man who stood guard, the one she thought might be Nigerian. He stood as if radiating potential—his magnificent head, solid, chiseled; his scalp shaved clean; his square jaw and radiant eyes that seemed to hold back some force to be reckoned with.

Now here he was, called into action and transformed in his running, his gaze and determination intent on something ahead of him. She felt the force of his passing, noticed how he held on to his walkie-talkie, both arms cutting into the air as if the maximize his ability to move, to warp space. Where had Ronald gone? She knew, from long experience, how he often separated from her at big exhibits like this. *Classic introvert*, he once confessed to her sheepishly, after she'd chided him for his tendency toward solitude. *It's just the way I process.*

She remembered that sweet, frowning smile he showed her whenever he made such a confession about himself. His *dachshund smile*, as she called it. She'd never shared this name with him; it was a private term of endearment she somehow felt the need to hold in reserve, so as to render it more precious, to protect it. She feared telling him would obliterate it, cause him to act on his self-consciousness and alter his expression and deny her one of the many subtle but enduring qualities that formed the foundation of her deep love for him.

That would be like him, she thought. He'd have just enough pride, or whatever the right word was, to banish the smile, to want to deny her an opportunity to infantilize him. *I'm so much older than you!* she could hear him, protesting in a kind of jest. *Why do you keep babying me?* And this brand of complaint, which she'd actually heard from him, in other contexts, also endeared him to her, enforced her lingering, fugitive vision of him as a boy . . . a grown-up boy with salt-and-pepper hair and a bit of a gut, but a boy nonetheless.

She turned to follow the guard. He'd long since disappeared but she could see a succession of startled visitors, looking after his wake in puzzlement, and then at each other, needing to confirm that something was going on. There were more voices far ahead, and as she got closer to them she saw people being ushered out of a gallery by other guards, their faces clearly written over with expressions of concern and fear. *An evacuation?* She remembered headlines about Paris, Monte Carlo, and various terrorist "soft targets," like museums, so ripe with potential. The news carried ripples of official concern on one side, sad resignation on the other, all borne along in the regrettable reality of risk fatigue.

Clumps of museum-goers shuffled past her. A white-haired woman, the very picture of a sensible pragmatist, seemed to read Lauren's confusion and offered helpfully, as she passed, "A medical emergency. They're asking us to leave the area."

But Lauren pressed on, determined to go as far as she could until one of the security people told her otherwise. She didn't want to leave without Ronald; they'd likely take too long to find each other outside (he always kept his cell phone off, with a Luddite persistence that annoyed her), so she made it a point to find him and head off any wasted time. She was hungry; they'd been ready for lunch about twenty minutes ago. Once ensconced in a nice café on the plaza, they could debrief as much as they needed, preferably after a glass or two of rosé and a fortifying lunch.

She found herself halted by a guard as she tried to peek into one of the galleries. She was about to turn away, assuming it had already been emptied, but over the uniformed man's shoulder, she saw something that made her insides heave—Ronald's green shirt, *on him*, as he lay spread across the gallery floor, surrounded by a group of concerned guards. At least three of them stood over him, most prominent among them, the assumed Nigerian, who was speaking urgently into his walkie-talkie.

I'm with him! She screamed, not realizing she would do so but suddenly glad of the power it gave her, and she broke past the man in the doorway, who was disarmed by her outburst. She ran to Ronald as the three guards turned wide-eyed expressions toward her, which almost immediately transformed into a kind of sad sympathy. Each of them stepped away to give her room, and soon she was bending over Ronald, realizing he was insensible, passed out, and she was barking questions at the men around her, imploring them to hurry, ignoring their reassurances. And then the weird blur of watching the paramedics race across the galleries toward her, toward the guards and Ronald, such an incredible image in itself, the gurney rattling past all those masterpieces.

The medics worked with rapid efficiency, first evaluating Ronald, then lifting him to the gurney, trying to reassure Lauren through her frantic questions, keeping Ronald in transit. In minutes, she was following them out, running with them, Ronald bundled, face now half-covered with one of those ugly, plastic oxygen masks. Into the warm air, with crowds of people watching, she was helped into the sudden hush of the ambulance interior and felt the lurch of it springing into speed. She kept her eyes upon Ronald's closed lids.

The hospital had been just as much of a blur.

A cardiologist, a fifty-something woman who radiated

enormous empathy, met her in a special waiting room off the ward after what had been an eternity for Lauren. She was grave, and informed Lauren that Ronald had suffered a massive coronary and was in a very precarious state. She did not look hopeful. The doctor had to return to the ward, and Lauren realized that she could not, not yet, call most of the friends and family she'd been thinking of. She first needed to know more. She spent her time looking but not looking out of the large waiting room windows at the city below. It was a beautiful warm day, the kind she and Ronald would have taken a long walk in, wandering their neighborhood shopping, or driving out to explore other parts of the city.

Almost two hours later, the doctor returned. For an instant, their eyes met across the distance of the long hallway, and then the doctor looked away quickly, as if mustering something. And it was then that Lauren knew. The doctor's words seared into Lauren's memory: ". . . I'm so sorry . . . there was nothing we could do for him. Do you have someone you can call, someone to be with you?"

And then Lauren was waking up in a room surrounded by nurses, having passed out. They dutifully took her blood pressure and other vitals, and the doctor checked in with her too, before Lauren was given the okay to go home. And where would she go? Her apartment, and all those now-dreaded, even horrible, reminders of Ronald's recent life? In her mind's eye, she could see the book he'd been reading, a fat history of the Weather Underground and the radicals of the '60s, still on his nightstand, with his spread-open reading glasses on top of it as if he'd just left the room. Already she was navigating these new emotional hazards of memory, the triggers waiting to send her spinning into grief's violent and relentless territories. She thought of their cat, Benton, watching the door for their return. Would he know, when it was just her, when she entered the apartment and broke down, that something irrevocable had transpired?

Eventually, of course, she had to go home, for Benton's sake, and she opened her doors, literally and figuratively, to the help of others. Over the next few weeks, a long line of her friends, Ronald's friends, as well as her own and Ronald's family, came with food, stayed the night, and did their best to help see her through the initial stages of shock, and then, mercifully, the intense release.

Until one day, she had to close the door to them and just pick up, resume what life she could. And she tried. But she knew it would take time. A lot of time. Her therapist had assured her of that. She remembered the day her father, a retired journalist, had taken her out for a long drive in his rented car. He'd visited her here enough to feel comfortable with the city and its environs. They both knew there was no destination, and no finish line for what she—what they—were going through. He drove over the bridge and into the outlying smaller towns north. Her father had been very fond of and close to Ronald, a bond that had always delighted her. Now the depth of their shared grief drew her closer to him, and reminded her of that dark period, during her graduate work, when her mother had died and she'd helped get him through that long mourning, which, like this one, had been hers as much as his.

Her father, a writer and a man of words, was wise enough to know the value of silence. Just being beside him in the moving car, even this unfamiliar one, made her feel as if she were enclosed within the comforts of the home she'd grown up in, the home he'd refused to leave, even after his wife's death and Lauren's eventual departure.

"They'll have to take me out of here toes first," he'd said to Lauren, and she'd laughed and chided him. "I'm serious," he declared. "It's one thing I won't surrender to, I don't care how many times everyone says this is 'too much house' for one person. And those drooling realtors . . . don't get me started! Bob Rinker has already asked me about the place *twice*!" She remembered her father's look of defiance as they sat there in his kitchen that day, sipping coffee and looking out the kitchen window at the vast back lawn, where she'd played as a child. It was covered with the red, yellow, and orange leaves of autumn.

Lauren had moved out, and on. Grad school, and then a series of jobs. She'd ended up on the West Coast.

She found herself continually amazed by the structure of her loss. Her therapy helped, but she found that most of her work at it, her slow, interminable accommodation to the great gulf she was swimming in, had to be taken on in solitude, and often, it was accompanied by anger. And bewilderment, even after many months. At a party, a year after Ronald's death, she was telling her friend Tim, "If one more person tells me how much they admire my strength, I'm going to strangle them. I haven't been strong. What is that, even? I've been ripped to the core. Every day is like an open wound. I've cried on the bus in front of strangers. It happened the other day. Sometimes they're sympathetic, but most of the time, they're scared. Can you blame them? Who wants to be captive to that much . . . emotion? Raw emotion." Tim had nodded in sympathy.

She remembered how one morning she actually had to get off the bus, it was so bad. She'd wandered into a park. It was on a hill, so she had a view of the city in the distance, and closer in, the beautiful modern, sloping tower of its main Catholic church, the Diocesan headquarters, and a modern architectural landmark that drew as many tourists as it did believers. Ronald had been Catholic; Lauren wasn't. She wasn't even sure she believed in anything spiritual. So she sat there, feeling cold on that park bench.

Looking around her, she'd experienced what she'd heard that many people in deep grief experience, those questions: *How can people around her go on with their lives? Wait in traffic? Talk to their dogs while walking them? Laugh with friends?* In the far distance, rising into the clear, blue morning, she watched the upward ascent of an airliner. The world was going on, and would go on. People were flying out into new journeys, chasing dreams, or careers. But maybe some, like her, were flying out through loss of one kind or another: breakups, stalled careers, and illness. Maybe some there were also bound toward sad, bereft family members and solemn ceremonies. The world continued, yes, but in *all* of its many aspects. This, perverse as it sounded, is what really gave her comfort. Her grief was hers, but she was not alone.

She moved through her days. As if to complement and amplify her grief, and add one more proof that the world could be terrifyingly redundant and random, a tangential friend of hers, Sheila, one of the large circle of women that Lauren met up with for Thursday evening drinking and dining parties, lost her fiancé in a startlingly, shockingly similar way to hers. It seemed to happen just as Lauren was feeling safely removed from the immediacy of her own experience.

Sheila had been home one afternoon cleaning when her cell rang. It was Norm's gym calling her, saying there'd been an emergency and that he'd been taken to the hospital, and Sheila had the same dazed journey and interval with doctors, the sudden death, the gut-wrenching pain of its abruptness, the expanse of a permanent loss that would never be eased by the solace of at least having the chance to say goodbye. In fact, when the gym had called, she thought it might be one of Norm's silly little jokes.

Lauren had duly visited Sheila, sat with her for hours on end, brought her food, and conversation, and what comfort she could. Mostly, it was listening. Often, just bearing the silence with Sheila in her apartment, which, for a long time, she could only bring herself to leave only for work or other obligations.

"I keep playing out that call, over and over," Sheila said blankly as they sat over coffee in her front room one morning. And then Lauren had been in that museum again, Ronald lying on that floor, his green shirt, and the guards. And she was nearly back in the immediacy of her own grief. She looked over at Sheila, and forced her rising emotions back for her friend's sake.

"I wish I could say that will go away, and maybe it will. In fact, it probably will, over time. Or at least, you'll sort of make a space for it. It won't ache as much," said Lauren as her friend looked at her through a mask that seemed to let both doubt and hope through, in equal measures. They became much closer because of the experiences they'd shared. And Lauren was gratified, they all were, in that circle, to see Sheila eventually emerge into life again. She'd never be the same, Lauren knew, just as she herself never would be. Still, there would be life again.

But life didn't have to continue in the same place or in some attempt to approximate what it had been, to hold on to the past, and to Ronald, that way. It had helped some who grieved, like her father, but Lauren knew she needed to move on, literally. Yes, she had her circle in the city, but the wider world called. She applied for research and teaching positions, and was eventually accepted for a post in Berlin. She knew German tolerably well, and had visited and loved the city, so it felt like a logical next step. And Ronald had so loved German beer . . . yes, he'd be going with her, in a way. The prospect of change energized her.

When she felt her plane lifting off for that last time, all the farewells behind her, she'd looked down onto the bright city, fading fast below her, and the shining bay, and she'd remembered that day in the park, when she'd been watching that departing plane. *My turn*, she said to herself as the pilot bore them up through the cloud cover, evening them out for the long trip to a new world.

She enjoyed the bustle of getting set up in a new home and job. About a year and a half after the move, settling in to her new life, she realized that her colleague Marvin was becoming a friend. More than a friend. She'd been charmed by his boyish demeanor and deference. What had started as a professional association slowly emerged into an intimacy, something they both regarded with a kind of hushed caution, and then an acceptance. He was younger than Ronald, close to her age (she could see Ronald sneering in mock indignation at her as she thought this). *Hush*, she said to him, and to herself, playfully. *It is time, after all.* She felt Ronald stepping back, in a noble acceptance and agreement. Marvin had been duly attentive to her story, clearly appreciating the person that Ronald had been in her life.

They'd had a decent interval of courtship. It was clear there was a future for them, and in due time, after nearly a year of dating, then living together, they were married. Her children, Gretchen, then Amelia, arrived over the next couple of years. She moved in with Marvin and her daughters into a new flat. The university granted her tenure.

Soon after that landmark, her friends Tim and Mason visited. It was November, and they were in the midst of a European tour, braving the weather for their first trip to the German capitol. She'd dutifully escorted them to the somewhat daunting, dizzying array of treasures to be found on Museum Island, an afternoon that left the three of them exhilarated and exhausted. The next day, they took a long walk through the glorious parks of the city's heart, to the famed Siegessäule, the Victory Column that, once they climbed its snaking stairwell, afforded a view of the autumnal splendor of the Tiergarten trees. They had dinner that evening in a cavern-ous, dim, and cozy restaurant, a local favorite she'd come to love. Sitting under its curved ceiling (what looked like an old tunnel) they enjoyed enormous beers, the performance of a folk band, and heaps of dinners that Tim and Mason were sure they could not finish, but did.

"So nice to be off the beaten path," said Tim. "We'd never have known about this place."

"It pays to have a good local guide," she said. "I can show you Charlottenburg tomorrow, if you'd like."

They nodded in eager assent; she could tell the beer had buzzed them a bit; she felt it herself. After the plates had cleared, they talked, relaxed by the comfortable, warm atmosphere of the place. Mason asked after the kids, if she planned to show them the US at some point, take them to San Francisco, tour at least some of the country the way their mutual friends, who'd moved to London and Oslo, had done.

"Eventually," she said. "Marvin and I are firm believers in the benefits of introducing kids to travel. Once they're big enough, that is. Marvin hasn't been in years, either. Except for a few academic conferences, but you don't really get to do much during those."

Somehow she found herself talking about Ronald. Perhaps it was a segue from her descriptions about her life with Marvin, how happy she was with him, and yet how the past, her past, had never really receded. Though she at times had thought so, she wasn't really one who believed in *putting things behind* her, and closing off whole chapters the way some people claimed to be able to do. If anything, her move to Berlin, her new career, her life with Marvin and the kids—all of these had combined to cast her life in the US in a more definitive light; the distance of time and miles had served to imbue it all with a deeper resonance, even a nostalgia.

"It's been, what, five years since Ronald?" said Mason.

"Six," she said, as he registered surprise. "Yeah, six. A bit longer, actually. But you know what," she said, looking at Tim and Mason in turn. "I still think about him *every day*. Every day. After all this time. And I ask myself, is it wrong? Is it somehow a betrayal of Marvin?"

She heard the two men, this loving couple, assuring her that it was nothing close to wrong. "There are no rules for grief," said Tim, gazing at her intently across the candlelit table. "There's no guidebook. No set time. I read recently that it takes at least two to three years for someone to process the death of a loved one . . . whatever 'process' means, right? But I think it takes even longer for some people."

"Was it that way with John," she asked, referring to Tim's former lover, who'd died of AIDS in the late '90s.

"God," said Tim, pausing, glancing away a moment. "Yeah. It still comes to me sometimes, just like I was right there again, right in the middle of it. Sometimes I have to stop and collect myself. Some image of him, especially one from those last days, will pop into my head. Or I'll see someone who reminds me of him. Out of nowhere, and there I am, back again."

Mason reached across the table to hold Tim's hand. Lauren watched the moment, heartened to hear Tim's description of how it had been, and how it sometimes still could be. It resonated deeply with how she felt now.

"At least I had some warning, with John," said Tim. "Yours was so sudden."

She shook her head, then felt the tears welling up. "I'm sorry," Tim said. "I didn't mean to open a wound." She could see that his own eyes, and Mason's too, had dampened.

"Please," she said. "Don't be. It's funny you should use that word. 'Wound.' It's how I think of it. It is a wound. But God, let's not get macabre," she said, mustering a chuckle and brushing a tear from her cheek. "I can just see Ronald rolling his eyes and making fun of me. That would be *so* him." Tim and Mason smiled. Ronald liked to be sarcastic.

They sat nursing their beers. There seemed to be no rush to get the check, no pressure from the wait staff for their table. She felt content and fortunate to have two old friends with whom she could share this communion. When the check did come, she deftly grabbed it, over their loud protests, and told them she'd wanted to give them this gift. Eventually, they relented, but only with great reluctance. She secretly loved playing with the dominant tendencies of men, but Tim and Mason were hardly the alpha male types. She thought again of Ronald, who, for all his easygoing tendencies, could certainly rise up with indignation in defense of his chosen territories. She missed him dearly. She walked with Tim and Mason out of the restaurant and along the broad boulevard, where they said their goodbyes for the evening, and went down into the U-Bahn station. On the ride back to her neighborhood, her mind wandered.

She remembered how, a week or so before she'd left for Berlin, she'd gone back to the museum. She'd needed to revisit the spot where Ronald had collapsed. She might as well say *died*. He'd been gone by the time they'd found him, his essence, his consciousness, in all likelihood, unavailable to her. Still, she'd whispered to him in the ambulance, hoping some semblance of him heard. She dreaded a return visit even though she knew that she needed to make it, that she, in fact, had wanted desperately to make it. She wasn't sure what her reaction would be, but she felt she had to finally confront it.

The building was much emptier. It was the middle of the week. Only small groups of people milled from gallery to gallery while guards stood by. She didn't recognize any of them. The handsome Nigerian was nowhere to be seen. She found the gallery, the corner where Ronald had been sitting, and breathed a sigh of relief when she saw that the bench, and the room, were both empty. She took a seat in front of the big canvas.

She leaned back to take the colorful painting in. It was enormous, dramatic even, measuring roughly fifteen feet long and about seven feet high. Across its length, a kind of off-white, cream background washed over in swaths of green, yellow, and bits of ochre and other colors. She thought of a jungle, a summer garden, or stand of flowers. She pictured a lawn party, a warm day, the taste of chardonnay or a rosé. Knowing that it had captivated Ronald made her linger and luxuriate in these associations, imagine him within the places it suggested to her.

It was funny, in all this time, she'd known nothing of the painting's details . . . the artist and the title . . . but now she read the placard beside it. It was called *Brava, Cassiopeia*. The artist was an Australian, Judith Whiteman. She checked the dates, saw that Whiteman was still alive, was now eighty-three. Lauren hadn't heard of her, but then again, beyond the American painters she loved, she wasn't particularly well-versed in contemporary non-American ones.

She imagined a picture of Whiteman, silver-haired and majestic in some sunny studio with huge windows, in Sydney, or Melbourne, or Perth. Or perhaps in a remote stretch of country. Australia had been initially settled by British convicts and their keepers, a penal colony. Was Whiteman descended from one of them? Was she still painting? Perhaps she could write to her. She believed an intimacy now bound them. A kinship. And this spot, here by Whiteman's grand painting, was now sacred, a kind of altar. She remembered hearing about Rothko's "chapel" in Austin, and how she'd long wanted to visit it.

She turned to take in the room, and was glad that it was still empty. *This will do*, she thought. She remained there for a long time, seated in front of the overwhelming canvas. She imagined Whiteman reading the letter that Lauren was now composing to her in her head.

You do not know me. It's very likely that we will never meet. But some years ago, something happened that I want you to know about. I am not an art "expert." My interest in it has always been what one could call passionate, but I do not know the language of art. I make no pretensions toward some deep understanding, some familiarity with "theory." Perhaps, as many artists do, you feel the same way. Art has offered me deep sustenance. I am a person of science, and yet I feel that you and I are now tied together in a profound way. I hope you will forgive me this confession. Your painting is embedded in my life . . . I will carry it with me always. From a very dark place, it has brought me light. Through a door that led me into a long night of intense pain, I have also found you, and the healing of your miraculous and shining day . . .

COLD FRONT

HE'D BEEN DEAD FOR a long time. Well, *that* part of him was. He couldn't remember when he'd last felt the old fire, the drive, libido, horniness—the synonyms arrayed in his mind like a vast comical list. The absence didn't bother him as much as his inability to summon to memory some sense, however imperfect, fleeting, or faded, of *how* it used to feel. It wasn't a matter of chronology as much as quality; if he could still access the essence of what it had been like, the physicality, the full body fusion, the way the cascade of multiple sensations used to wash over him in his youth, then he'd be able to revel in the feeling, or some version of it.

Sometimes hints of the memory of his old body would return to him, like that almost beatific moment at that resort in Palm Springs a few years ago, when some passing scent in the air—weirdly suggestive of his Midwestern youth—brought him back to his thirties again, to being beautiful under that golden sun. Because he *had* been beautiful, back then.

And so went the run of Harlan's thoughts at this late date. Funny how these meditations took such a full form, even eloquence, as he navigated those most basic of tasks, those little errands that now constituted his routine. Gone were the days of cramped underground commutes to the Financial District, a neatly folded *Wall Street Journal* apprising him of developments that governed his professional choices, his clients' lives, and the trust under which he held them. These days his young (and often annoyingly cocky) successors used those compact little electronic screens. They could even listen to music or watch TV on them; he'd seen that on Muni recently and muttered a sarcastic *mirabile dictu* under his breath.

Now here he was, ruminating again, still recovering from his slog up the hill to his neighborhood market. Those three blocks hadn't always been a problem. Lately they winded him. *Well, that's the chemo*, he said to himself. In one short year his body had had to accommodate the shock of diagnosis, then the treatments, weight loss, and, unexpectedly, a disturbing shift in his palate. Many of his favorite foods were subtly changed, devoid of pleasure now. It was just one of his many diminishing senses, one that bothered him more than his nonexistent hunger for erotic connection. In truth, there was a small blessing in his now chilled capacity for lust. It had been drifting in that direction for years. Frankly, it made things easier.

So when he turned the corner into the produce aisle, he wasn't prepared for what he saw, and felt. A bolt. There along a wall of green—the chard, chives, artichokes, asparagus, arugula, etc., the automatic mister just beginning its gentle hiss—stood a young man, tall and slender, Latin, and exceedingly beautiful. He was at work, busily resupplying the depleted supply of cilantro. For the moment, they were alone, and Harlan couldn't help himself from staring at him. And the young man saw, noticed his gaze, read its import, and gave a slight, tired smile, as if to say, *Oh well, another one.*

Harlan quickly recovered himself. He abhorred rudeness, and he could not let himself become a *Lecherous Leering Old Man*. He resumed shopping.

Later, his tote bags unpacked, he rested in his flat. His cell phone rang, blaring its loud approximation of an old rotary phone. No chirps or song snatches for him. He saw the name—Brandon— floating there. This young man, a jovial Filipino with a winning smile, was his caretaker. Harlan might have been able to still get along without someone like Brandon, but he thought it wise to forge the relationship now, for when he really *did* need it.

"Hey" he heard, amused as always that Brandon talked to him in such a decidedly *young* way.

"Hey yourself," said Harlan. "I just ran to the market earlier, so I think we're covered, but it's always lovely to hear from you."

"You sure?" said Brandon.

"Yes, it's always quite lovely . . ."

"No, silly! I meant, 'You sure you don't need anything else?' I've got the car. We could even just go for a ride, maybe out to Lands End. It's gorgeous out!"

"I noticed," Harlan said. Just as he did said it, as he glanced down from his second-story window. he saw a gaggle of young men, most with beards, so *de rigueur* these days, approaching along the sidewalk just under him, sporting stylish shorts, preppy-looking shirts, and expensive shades.

"So let's go then?" said Brandon. It was less a question than a challenge.

Harlan sighed. Did he want to? He decided it would be better, said yes, and a mere fifteen minutes later, he lowered himself into Brandon's coffee-colored hatchback, and soon they were buzzing along on their way.

As Brandon drove them across town and made the approach to the Golden Gate, Harlan found himself dozing. But he perked up when they approached the span, those big reddish towers majestic and bright in the afternoon. Brandon hummed along with some music he was streaming, and Harlan looked at the tourists, the joggers, and the cyclists making their way across the narrow passages on either side of the traffic. It always seemed crowded here. He thought he'd heard Brandon say they were heading to the Marin Headlands, and the idea lifted him. He hadn't been along there in ages, and the prospect of those sweeping views was a sight, he realized now, that he'd long missed.

The little car dutifully wound around, up and down, and it

wasn't long before the vast stretches of the sunlit Pacific shimmered below and extended out and away from them. It was almost as if they were floating, as if the planet had pulled back a big blanket to remind them of just how small they were. The road was theirs; almost no other cars approached or lingered behind them.

Harlan tried to remember the last time he'd been out this way. There had been his boyfriend, Carl, all those years ago, and their treks—picnic supplies and white wine in a basket—to Black Sands Beach and other choice spots along the coast.

"Is Black Sands still a nude beach?" Harlan asked, surprising Brandon a bit, who raised an eyebrow with a studied, comic leer.

"Uh, yeah. Last time I checked."

Harland giggled. "I won't ask . . . "

"It's okay if you do."

"Oh, I had my day in the sun, believe me. I suppose you have too, and still are having it, I hope. That's all well and good, but we can leave it at that."

"Whatever you say," said Brandon, softly laughing.

Before Harlan knew it or could ask, Brandon had slowed and angled off the road to a little parking area where one or two other cars were lined. There was no one in sight.

"Feels like a good time for some fresh air," said Brandon. "But don't worry . . . we're not climbing anywhere."

"As if I could," said Harlan. "But yes, the sun and the breeze would do my old bones and lungs some good." And they did. Once he'd managed to rise up out of the cradle of the compact, Harlan found himself glad his young friend had made all this effort.

He was surprised at how quiet it was here. He ambled close to the edge of some low wildflowers that bordered the spot where the path to the beach, far below, began. The bright, sunny afternoon over the ocean lay beyond, and the far-off bridge carried its lines off to the left, little glints of traffic visible along its deck.

And then, strangely, Harlan was waking up.

For a second, he had no idea where he was or what was

happening. A voice came to him urgently through his haze. Eventually he recognized it as Brandon's and he realized that he must have passed out. Brandon had, one way or another, managed to get Harlan comfortably positioned on the ground and had either revived him, or had simply fretted and shaken him until he'd come around. It was, of course, alarming for both of them, though perhaps more so for Brandon.

Harlan felt strangely calm. "Well, I'm not sure I'm all that happy about *that*," he joked.

"I am pretty sure that I am definitely *NOT* happy about it. Jesus Har, are you okay?!?"

Harlan looked up, touched by his friend's concern, and gently patted his shoulder reassuringly. "Right as rain," he said. "Don't you worry. Though maybe it is best that we go back."

Brandon helped him into the car. Once behind the wheel, he turned to look again at Harlan, his face still deep with concern.

"Are you *sure*?" he asked.

Harlan extended his arm, finger pointing. "Drive," he said.

"Uh, just so you know, you're pointing to the ocean. I'm not going all *Thelma and Louise* for you."

"Drive the fuckin' car!" said Harlan, playfully swatting at him. Relieved, Brandon got them back in motion.

There was a fair amount of traffic in the city, so it took a bit longer to get to Harlan's place. At one point, waiting at an intersection on Geary Street, the long artery that almost bisected the whole of the city, Harlan saw a supermarket and remembered his vision of that beautiful young man in the produce aisle. It felt less ordained now, less a vision, and more of a *memento mori*. He muttered the Latin phrase to himself, but it must have emerged without any conscious realization, because Brandon, still alert for anomalies of any kind, started a little.

"What??" he asked.

It took Harlan a few beats to realize what he'd said. "Oh, yes. That. A bit of Latin." He looked over at Brandon, who still seemed puzzled.

"You went to St. Ignatius, right?" he asked Brandon. "Didn't those Jesuits teach you *any* Latin?"

"They don't really do that anymore . . ."

"What I said was 'memento mori', which is a fancy way of saying 'Remember, you're gonna die.'"

"Well, here's something not so fancy—would you *shut up?!*"

Harlan wasn't sure if he was touched or alarmed that Brandon was now upset. A little of both, he supposed. "I'm sorry," he said. "I guess it's a bad joke, though I wasn't really joking. Hey, it scared me too, kiddo."

"Let's just get you home," said Brandon.

Later that week, Brandon made sure to shuttle Harlan to his oncologist. They'd gone to the ER the afternoon of the incident, as a precaution, and had been told Harlan was likely suffering from dehydration, a conclusion Harlan's oncologist eventually agreed with. He was given a sheaf of instructions to help him eat properly and stay hydrated, and sent on his way. Brandon made it a point to check on him more often, so Harlan got used to more phone calls, and a few more visits than he'd had before.

And so they fell into a kind of routine to the point where, one Thursday morning, Harlan suddenly realized that he hadn't heard from Brandon in a day or so, which was unusual. He called Brandon's cell and got his clipped but breezy little greeting. When the beep sounded, he left a message that came off as perhaps a little too concerned. But he let it stand, and tried not to worry.

When it was later in the day and he still hadn't heard from Brandon, Harlan called the care service, but he had to leave a message there too. Less than an hour later, they called back. A kind-sounding agent spoke with him.

"We're very glad you called, Mr. Marrison," the man said. "Would you be able to come in to see us this afternoon? Our office is close to you, but we could have someone pick you up."

Harlan tried to keep an even tone through what he realized was a steadily building alarm. "Well, yes, I certainly can . . . but is everything okay?"

"There's no reason to worry, Mr. Marrison. But it would be best if we could talk with you in person. We have some paperwork we need you to update, so if you could come down, we'll be more than happy to see you right away. Ask for me. My name is Benjamin."

"And I'm Harlan . . . but I guess you knew that."

A friendly and endearing chuckle. "Of course. I look forward to seeing you . . . does one-fifteen work?" Harlan said yes and hung up, grabbing his jacket to head out.

When Harlan arrived, a slender balding man with an extraordinarily kind face approached him and led him to an enclosed office in the back of the suite. He offered Harlan one of two comfortable chairs along the window beside his desk, and sat across from him in the other.

"I do, unfortunately, have some bad news," he said, leaning forward. "Brandon's been in a car accident. It was serious. He's at SF General right now, but they're going to transfer him to a special neurological facility in the North Bay later this week. Brandon is in and out of consciousness. I've spoken to his doctors many times now," and here Benjamin stopped, bowing his head briefly. When he faced Harlan again, his eyes glistened.

"They're reasonably confident that Brandon is going to pull out of this, but these things, especially with potential brain injuries . . . well, I guess you already know they can be tricky."

Harlan let it all sink in. Through the window behind Benjamin, he could see the rooftop of a building that he realized was the home of a longtime neighborhood Italian restaurant, a place he'd frequented since he'd first moved to the area in the early 1970s. Why in God's name he should be thinking of all that now he had no idea. But somehow those memories of comfort and old friendships made him saddened all the more at this news about Brandon. He struggled to suppress a sob. Benjamin regarded him with a look of reassuring patience and empathy.

"Can I see him?"

Benjamin sighed. "I asked them that too. Unfortunately, we can't just yet. Not with the transfer coming. But they'll let us know as soon as we can and I promise you, I will not only let you know, but we can go together if you'd like. It's in Marin."

Harlan looked at him, unable to speak again but nodding a silent and grateful agreement. He found himself taking to Benjamin immediately. Recovering himself, he thanked him, offered his hand, and they shook as he rose to leave.

"Call me if you need anything," Benjamin said. "No matter the time. As much as you need to. Can I get you a ride home?"

"Thank you so much, for all of this," said Harlan. "I can walk home, but thank you."

Back out on the street, Harlan moved in a kind of daze. He was still reeling from the news. It upended his view of his friendship with Brandon, and his sense of the world, of reality . . . even of justice. Because he'd never seen Brandon as anything but young and vital (in addition to loving and kind). This was all the more the case because Harlan had come to accept himself as "old" and "sick" and, therefore, somewhat compromised, past his "due date" (if he were to be true to his native dark humor and cynicism). How could such misfortune befall someone so markedly undeserving of it? It was, in fact, a cruel turn of fate, the blackest of jokes that seemed directed at Harlan himself, as if to goad him. Very well, he was goaded, and angry.

He found himself suddenly wanting to shout. He passed a young homeless man begging for money and, to his eyes now, seemingly awash in self-pity. Harlan nearly stopped to give this youth a piece of his mind. Fortunately he checked the urge; he'd seen, all too often, how violent street people can become, and, as he considered it further, you really never know anyone's story.

Realizing now just how chaotic the swirl of emotions within

him had become, Harlan stopped in front of a shop to catch his breath and collect himself. He had only the dimmest awareness of what was in the window in front of him. It looked like a gift boutique . . . bright ceramics, fancy cocktail implements and the like. What actually caught his eye was his own reflection. *Well how do you feel now?* he wanted to ask it. A phrase he'd read long ago, in a favorite literary essay, floated into his mind: *The life sentence of the mirror.* Yes, it is a sentence, of sorts, but he'd long ago made peace with his. All the familiar components were there. Harlan had not become one to fight the advances of age. He, quite resolutely, had never used hair dye. He didn't even think about trying to wage war on any wrinkles, though he did moisturize and use sunscreen regularly. And he'd never, ever considered those obscene machines that literally suck the fat out of burgeoning midsections.

Calmer now, he resumed his walk home, thinking of Brandon all the way. Eventually, a week or so later, he got that call from Benjamin. They drove to Marin (a trip, of course, fraught with reminders of that increasingly distant-feeling day with Brandon). Brandon was in and out of awareness when they'd visited him, from the painkillers, but Harlan managed a tearful hello, and came away from the visit bolstered by a very kind doctor's assessment that his friend would likely face a long recovery, but would be okay. And the irony of the both of them now being convalescent, in a sense, was not lost on him. Benjamin made sure Harlan had a new caregiver, who was competent and kind. But he was alas, no Brandon, Harlan joked to himself.

One night a few weeks after his first visit with Brandon, Harlan had a notably vivid dream, one that left him emotionally shaken upon waking. He was working as toll taker on a bridge. He assumed it was the Golden Gate Bridge, but the details were murky, the locale indistinct, and a think fog enveloped nearly everything beyond his toll station. All he could really see was the approach of each car as it emerged from the wall of thick fog and rolled to a stop beside his booth, as if fresh from some heaven or underworld.

Each car was filled with beautiful young people, invariably giddy, smiling, and carefree. They'd hand their fare to him and then glide blithely on. When Harlan reached out to take their money, the cool air chilled his forearm. The parade seemed endless. Then it seemed to stop. No more cars. He became alarmed. Nervously, he looked at his fellow toll takers, but each one seemed unconcerned with this new development. One was reading a book. Another tapped his desk, as if drumming to music.

Harlan heard a car approaching in his lane. It was a navy blue 1968 Oldsmobile with a white cream, buff top. A convertible. He'd inherited this car from his father, back in Akron, and had driven it in his twenties. It was a handsome car, and it bore memories of many a carefree summer night.

It rolled dutifully to a stop, and the young man at the wheel turned to look at him, making no move to offer any money for the fare. In fact, he made no move at all. He simply stared at Harlan. It was his own, youthful self, the beautiful young man he'd once been. They sat watching each other. Harlan wanted to say something to him, but when he opened his mouth, he had nothing. No sage advice. No admonitions to make better use of his time. No warnings that the looks wouldn't last. After a minute, his younger self turned away and drove on, disappearing into the fog.

Harlan sat watching the now-empty road that led into the city, the same route that had swallowed all those other cars of the youthful. In the distance behind him, and for the first time, it seemed, Harlan heard the plaintive, claxon warnings of the bridge's foghorns. He then realized that they had been sending out their persistent warnings, slowly and steadily, all this time.

CITY OF MEMORY

ALLEN HAD SEEN IT all. Or at least, a lot of it.

Like those two suicides off the Golden Gate Bridge. It was during his temporary directorship of that theater company in Marin, the only real "commute" he'd ever had. Two jumpers in the space of a little over a year. Some people had, maybe, seen one. Many never saw any. The images of both were burned into his mind. They would be, forever. The tiny white-haired elderly woman with the purple raincoat. The young Asian man, with the black pants and vividly bright sneakers. The young man had paused, twirling curiously in a little circle on the walkway before he leapt and jumped. The woman never hesitated at all, and simply approached the railing, gripped it, and heaved herself up and over in a surprisingly spry leap. He remembered that brief flash of purple, then the empty air over the red bridge railing.

He'd seen four US Presidents. That included Gerry Ford during the attempted assassination outside the Sir Francis Drake Hotel in '76. There'd been Nixon. And Carter. Both at campaign stops. He'd hooted at the former, cheered the latter. Reagan too, during that protest in the '80s. He'd really shouted at *him*. They all did. What was that chant? Something about how the President had never even said the word "AIDS." But the man simply flashed his famous smile as he vanished into the arena. That was before poor, crazy, lovelorn Hinckley shot him. Despite his antipathy toward the President, Allen had been glad he'd survived.

A lot for one life, Allen thought, and more death than he cared to remember, between Vietnam, and then AIDS. Those were the years when the city was steeped in death, almost like you could smell it on the wind blowing through the Castro. Death. And fear, a weary fear, on all the faces along the sidewalks. Yes. A lot more than he cared to remember, and God knows there was a lot he'd probably forgotten by now, but the mark of all of it certainly made him feel that his own life was all the more precious.

He drove along Ocean Beach, and those signature opening chords of Buffalo Springfield, "For What It's Worth," came on, and took him back. *Talk about timing*, Allen thought, as he turned up the volume. *Something happening here*, indeed. Well, there *used* to be something happening. The Haight in '67, the famous Summer of Love and all those literal "happenings"—the Diggers, the poets. What was his city now? All tech boom and too much money. Much too much money.

He was taking the roundabout way, a little drive around the edge of the city to clear his head before he met with his new potential landlord over at Rincon Hill. Like a lot of people, Allen was being forced out of his old place. He still made a good living from his residuals. Yes, he'd been an actor, a "character" actor to be precise, one of those faces you see in movies all the time. Mostly minor speaking roles (except for a few independent arthouse films, in which he was a lead or a supporting role). And commercials too— he'd once had a specialty in "headache relief" medicines, something about his face that suggested a man who suffered migraines.

The money had been good, and for the most part, it still was. He'd aged into a new category of white male desirability: he'd been a doctor, lawyer, and detective many times over. He'd been onscreen with Harrison Ford as a doomed thug/guard in one of the *Indiana Jones* films. He'd worked with Connery too, as in Sean, and Hackman, as in Gene.

He neared the Ferry Building, along the stretch of road that used to be the double-decker Embarcadero, before it came down after the Loma Prieta quake in '89. How many of the tourists and techies, now walking amid the lunch crowd along the bright and breezy Embarcadero, were even *alive* in '89? *Easy Allen*, he thought. *You were young once too. Don't become a cliché.* "I am cliché!" he said aloud as he drove along. The sight of the Bay and the sunny afternoon and the crowds suddenly put him in a festive mood. "A big, fat, flourishing cliché!" Buffalo Springfield had given way to the Turtles, then the Moody Blues, and now, the easy sounds of Marvin Gaye's, "What's Goin' On?"

At a stoplight, with the Bay Bridge looming to his left, Allen pulled out the slip of paper with the address he needed. He still wrote things down, even though he had one of the smart phones, and did, in fact, use it now and then, he had little trust of cyberspace, or more specifically, The Cloud. Paper still worked just fine, thank you very much.

115 Pima Lane. He'd never heard of it. Parking somewhere off of Harrison, he fished out his phone, sighing as he put on his cheaters and punched in the address for his destination on Google Maps. He guessed Pima was one of the many obscure alleys and lanes that poked out like porcupine quills on the street map of the Rincon Hill area. He found it, lifted himself out of his Mazda, and began the walk, a pulsing blue dot on his phone screen assuring him that he made progress, albeit slowly, but progress nonetheless. Pima ended up being a tiny sliver of an alley ("lane" was far too grandiose) almost under the Bay Bridge at the base of Rincon, a setting that might seem ominous to many, with that great, traffic-thundered steel bulk overhead. Allen decided it was charming. He liked the looks of it, and took that as a good omen. Allen believed in omens.

"Mr. Richards," said the voice on the intercom after he buzzed it, more of a statement than a question. The gate buzzed and he walked into a small courtyard, a little surprised that at such a short distance from the street he felt like he was in an oasis of solitude. It was an older brick building, but one responsibly braced and earthquake-retrofitted by black-painted steel, a look not uncommon in this part of the city, and it reassured him.

Allen had been given the name of Mr. Lee, the landlord, by one of his former casting agents, who was well connected in town. Lee, he'd been given to understand, liked to support the arts community, and Allen, though he didn't quite think of himself as an artist, was willing to take the label if it meant a good place to live at an affordable price.

"Quite different from the Castro, yes?" Lee stood in the courtyard, a trim Chinese man in his early sixties, wearing a navy-blue blazer and khakis, somewhat more formal than Allen had expected, but the overall effect was of a studied and at-ease professionalism. *Seems like an honest broker*, was Allen's initial thought. Lee led him efficiently into the unit, smoothing the process with a pleasant patter that offered helpful details about the property.

"Very private, you see," said Lee, "and, you will find, quiet too." He walked to the main window at the end of the primary room, pulled a cord to open the blinds, revealing a more-than-passably pleasing vista of the bridge, the Bay beyond. "Excellent view, as you can see."

Allen was still regarding the view as Lee enumerated the kitchen appliances, noted the in-unit washer/dryer, the built-in shelves, and the small half bath. It was overall, well maintained, gloriously spacious, and, in a word, perfect for Allen. He was almost afraid to ask the price, but Lee offered a monthly amount that seemed surprisingly good. He hated using a cliché, but then again, he was one. "What's the catch?" he asked, laughing at his own joke but holding Lee's gaze pointedly, intent on provoking any red flags that might be in hiding, to show themselves.

Lee chuckled good-naturedly, getting Allen's joke. "None,

I assure you Mr. Richards, though I certainly understand your position," he said. "As I believe your friend has told you, I have an interest in providing for people such as yourself. This city, as you know, has become quite unlivable for many. And trust me, I am very selective. You come well recommended, and I trust our mutual friend." He paused, letting Allen digest his words.

"I will give you a chance to look around. If you have any questions, I will be just outside. Please, Mr. Richards, take your time."

Allen could hardly believe his good fortune, how easily and quickly this opportunity had come his way. He'd had friends who gave up on finding a new property in the city and had long since decamped to Oakland, Pleasanton, and even farther afield. He detected no hint of pressure from Lee, yet he still felt as if he should act soon.

He paced along the finely maintained hardwood floor of the main room, noticed the small but comfortable looking terrace outside the big window (Lee hadn't even mentioned it—talk about a soft sell). He imagined his furniture and how it would be arranged, noted the vast southern wall, perfect for his bookcases and ample library. The kitchen, more than satisfactory. The main bedroom, cozy with beams and exposed brick.

Lee was bowed over his phone, presumably, his back to Allen, when the latter had exited the apartment. Sensing a presence behind him, Lee turned. "To your liking, I hope?" he asked, neither eager nor presumptuous.

"More than to my 'liking,'" Allen replied. "But I have to ask: Did anyone die in that place?"

"Certainly not while I have owned the building, Mr. Richards. But then, I can't speak for any time before that."

"I was mostly joking," said Allen. "It just seems like such a great opportunity. I figured there had to be some catch."

"Understandable," said Lee, exuding calm.

Allen turned to survey the surroundings, and then again, turned back to Lee. "Where do I sign?"

Allen's old friend Brenda came along with Duke, another friend, though a newer one, on the day Allen moved in. Brenda had moved with Allen to the city, from Toledo, way back in the early '60s, something Duke, not yet thirty, found wondrous.

"Was the world actually black and white back then?" Duke had once joked, the first time he'd met Brenda and had been forced to listen to one of her and Allen's "remember-when?" conversations.

Brenda had been there when Ginsberg first read "Howl" at that gallery (she later drove Duke past the site)—all of this instantly endearing her to Duke, an aspiring writer. Duke had met Allen at a poetry workshop, an event Allen had attended because the guy he was dating at the time was leading it. That guy didn't last. Duke did.

"Not your usual type," Brenda had said at the time, and Allen could tell that she appreciated Duke's blonde good looks and jock physique as much as he did.

"It's not about *that*," he said to her, and, seeing the mock-doubtful cast of her eyes, added, "No, really. It's not."

"Okay either way," she said. "Truly. I'm just glad you have someone new in your life."

Allen had appreciated that she said someone "new" and not just "someone." He knew she'd worried about him. Between death and relocation, the attrition among his friends had been hard to bear over the last ten years. He never said as much, but she knew, and he knew she knew. That was enough.

After one relatively undemanding day of moving, the furniture and boxes were all in. While Duke went out to return the U-Haul (which, fortunately, was not far at all), Brenda ordered Chinese takeout, then uncorked the Robert Mondavi Pinot Noir she'd brought.

"I mean," she said, as if already warmed by the wine, "we've got to do that Chinese-takeout-on-the-floor routine for your first night in the place, am I right?"

"In case you didn't know it," Allen said, "I revel in cliché. It's one of the epiphanies that this move has prompted."

Brenda looked around, nonplussed, not getting the joke. "Never mind," Allen said. "Count me as very happy to be here."

And he was, he had no doubt. But that first night in the new place had been difficult, as in, strange. As in waking up at around 3:00 a.m. and suddenly being freaked out by the unfamiliar layout of the bedroom, the particular play of shadows on the wall, the complete absence of the voices of bar revelers, stumbling home, carrying in through his window as they always had outside his Castro flat.

They'll probably rent that place for $3,500 now, easy, he said to himself, sighing in his old bed in that new room. He remembered Lee's patter. *Not the Castro* indeed. It might as well have been another country. He'd started to think of it all, the years back there, wondering what this change meant. Would he find himself encamped in some Castro café, a tourist in his old neighborhood? There wasn't much of a neighborhood here, one of the few drawbacks of the new place. One or two corner stores within a block or two. And the YMCA, the old one, was his new gym. He could walk there. That was about it. He'd need the Mazda, or Muni, to take him anywhere else.

He'd nearly drifted off when he heard something. He wasn't sure what. Did he dream it? Not a thump, no "bump in the night," but more like . . . what the hell? It had to be pre-sleep. What do they call it, the "hypnagogic" state? He sometimes, in that same zone, had heard the voice of his mother, or his father, both long dead. But "hearing" them always put him at ease. He was alert now, but not enough to get out of his warm bed to investigate. And soon, anyway, he was asleep.

The next night, after a day of unpacking, Allen fell asleep much more easily. But his slumber was not uninterrupted. Sometime in the very early morning something called him back from his dreams. A voice. This time, most definitely, a voice. For a second, he simply thought he was, as he always had been, in his old flat. Then he remembered.

He walked tentatively down the hall from his bedroom to the front. Had it come from here? Maybe a homeless camp or a random crazy person? He peeked through the blinds but could only see the lights of the Bay Bridge, shining in milky light through the fog. No other sound. Dead silence. He grabbed a quick glass of water and headed back to bed.

In the morning, after breakfast and showering, he walked outside the courtyard gate, and found some steps leading down the slope to the base of the building, where he thought the voice had come from. These led to a small lightly grassy slope leading from the building's foundation to a high chain-link fence. On either side of it, nothing but windblown litter, small bits of paper, coffee cups, some plastic bottles. But no sign of any encampment or recent habitation. All the surrounding buildings looked light industrial: warehouses, auto body shops, and the like. Allen chuckled to himself. Big city, he thought. Who knows what goes on in the middle of the night.

Taking out the trash one day, Allen was startled to find Mr. Lee in the courtyard. He hadn't really seen anyone else since he'd been in his new place. The other tenants seemed invisible. Lee was uncharacteristically dressed in jeans and a gray athletic sweater, and somewhat dirty-looking clothes at that. He carried a toolbox.

"Good morning, Mr. Richards," he said, waving. Allen had decided not to ask Lee to address him in more familiar terms. He liked Lee's courtly formality. No one else, after all, called him "Mister."

"I do have a question," said Allen, strolling over to Lee. "Or more of statement, I guess. You don't really have a homeless problem around here, people camped out nearby, that sort of thing?"

"No," said Lee. "I can't say you won't see an occasional homeless person walking through the area, but I certainly haven't seen any camps or anything of that nature. Have you?"

"No, me neither," said Allen. "Just curious. Thanks." He

started to walk back, then stopped. "It's just that I heard some voices. Outside. Last night. Some shouting."

Lee nodded, looking thoughtful but not concerned. "Please do let me know if you hear any more. If it becomes a problem, I can look into it."

Allen responded with a smile and a quick "thanks" and went back inside.

About a week or so later Allen was awakened again in the middle of the night, only this time, from something more prosaic: a good old-fashioned thunderstorm. They were rare in the Bay Area, and Allen actually relished them, since they were a palpable reminder of his childhood in Ohio. He lay awake watching the play of the lightning and listening to the rumbling and boom of the thunder, and the windswept rain as it drove at the windows. God, he missed it. Across town, Brenda must have been thinking the same thing.

Some of the thunder was intense. Allen decided to watch the storm from his front windows, so he padded down the hall and carefully opened the blinds. He stood and watched the storm for a while. Eventually it seemed to die down, move on. He shuffled to his kitchen island to get some water. He took a few sips. Put down the glass. He felt a distinct chill on his neck, almost like a breeze. Then he swore he heard a voice.

Are you ready?

He started, turned around in a flash, heart racing. No one. Nothing. He looked around the room. Then he ventured cautiously down the hall, passing his bathroom and checking it, then the bedroom, then back to the front. He stood at the island. He was rattled, not sure he could go back to sleep.

Without making coffee or showering, he dressed in a kind of daze, grabbed his keys, and was soon in his Mazda, braving the morning chill to make his way to his favorite twenty-four-hour diner in the Castro. Likely full of out-all-night club kids at this point, he thought, but he felt like he needed some human contact, and it was too early to wake up Brenda.

After a very satisfying omelet and a few cups of coffee, Allen felt a little better. There were indeed a few club kids scattered among the booths behind him and their gleeful chatter helped too. It was still too early to hit up Brenda; he knew she was decidedly in the not-a-morning person camp. So he decided to stroll the streets of what was now his old neighborhood.

He turned off 17th St. onto Castro St., the main thoroughfare, passing "Twin Peaks," the neighborhood's last "real" bar, Allen thought. It had great Irish coffee, but it was too early for that too. He stopped in front of the grand old Castro Theater, perusing the coming attractions posters. Back in the day he'd gone to so many movie nights here. His jovial band of friends would take over a section of seats and hurl up campy catcalls at *The Exorcist* and *Mommie Dearest*. In his opinion, both were classics.

He walked on. At the intersection of Eighteenth and Castro, he paused again. He'd seen the storefronts in this neighborhood change so many times over the last forty-plus years that he'd lost track of what had been what back then. Lots of old favorite bars had come and gone, and the spirit of the place had changed somewhat. He turned off onto Nineteenth, heading north: his favorite coffee spot after all these years. And Isaac's antique shop, which was there when Allen and Brenda had first landed in the Castro, still going strong. At the corner of Collingwood by the Harvey Milk school, he finally decided to call Brenda.

"Hey," she said, almost tenderly. "Early for me, yes, but for you too. What's up?" He gave her a quick rundown, as much as he could muster without giving her too much detail. "Better come over," she said.

Brenda lived in a mansion on the corner of Caselli and Douglass, a gorgeous behemoth that had once been a hospital, sometime in the late nineteenth century, when most of the neighborhood was still rolling hills. The huge building had long ago been carved up into separate units, each one unique. Brenda's was in one of the mansion's circular towers, on the second story, her curved front window affording an eastern view, neighborhood rooftops, and far off, the Oakland hills.

She led him to the couch, where a coffee was waiting for him. "Damn, I've had a lot already," he said, taking the warm cup. "But a little more won't hurt."

"So you honestly don't think it was a dream?"

"God, I wish I it was," he said. "But I was wide awake and drinking water. I swear I heard it. And then there was that draft on my neck. Don't they always say that, in ghost stories, how ghosts make it colder? I can't explain it."

"I'm guessing you've already thought about that question. As in 'ready for what?' right?"

"I know! I mean, talk about creepy!"

"A classic haunting, I'd say." She took a sip of her coffee and looked out her window. Allen didn't like how easily she came to that conclusion.

"And Lee never said anything about the place?" she asked. "I think there's actually a law where landlords need to tell prospective tenants if there's any history of spooky stuff," she said. Allen nodded no.

Brenda offered to let him spend the night at her place, and he actually took her up on it. He went down to Walgreens later to pick up a toothbrush and a few other things, warming to the idea of a good old-fashioned sleepover. She made dinner and invited Duke.

"So, hearing voices now?" said Duke as they sat over their empty plates and still-full wine glasses. Brenda had set them up in her front room. Outside, gold lights in the houses gleamed through the fog enshrouding Eureka Valley.

"I'm not schizoid if that's what you're implying," said Allen, grinning.

Duke nodded, "Fair enough. But what I mean is, well, you're sure?"

"So dude," said Duke, looking at Allen. "Would it help if I slept over at your place? Are you still freaked out?"

Across from Allen, Brenda grinned. He tried to ignore it as best he could. Her gentle teasing about his love life over the years sometimes annoyed him, but it never rose into the realm of argument or rancor. He allowed her those little gibes. It looked like Duke hadn't caught on to Brenda's coy teasing. If he did, he pretended not to notice.

Allen looked off, seriously considering Duke's offer. "Yeah, to the question about whether I'm freaked out, an emphatic yes, but I think I have to face this on my own. But if I show up at your door at some point tomorrow night, you'll know why."

"Deal," said Duke.

"Maybe you should get the place blessed," said Brenda. "The church still does that, you know."

A couple of days later, after hanging out with Duke in the Haight, Allen walked from the Panhandle, over the hill and back to the Castro. He was heading to Holy Redeemer Church, but he needed to walk back and forth more than a few times before he worked up the nerve to push the doorbell outside of the pastor's residence. He heard it ringing deep within. A long pause, then eventually, the gate buzzed and the door at the top of the steps opened tentatively. A sixty-something man in layperson's clothes looked down quizzically as Allen explained that he needed to talk to the pastor, or the deacon, or someone, if it was at all possible. The man nodded and opened the door wider, beckoning Allen in.

He told Allen to have a seat in a waiting room that was a living room. Once settled in, Allen was lulled to relative calmness by the homey atmosphere, and the steady ticking of a nearby grandfather clock. A portrait of Jesus—that improbably Anglo-Saxon, model-handsome, bearded variety of Our Savior—smiled down from above the fireplace. *One of the Brothers Gibb*, thought Allen. *Maybe Andy? Or Barry?*

Within minutes, the pastor stepped in, a genial white-haired man. Father Donnely introduced himself and walked Allen to his office down the hall. Allen told his story the best he could. Father Donnely listened patiently, his expression even.

"So you're wondering if I, or the Church, can do something?" he asked Allen.

"Well, I guess. I thought I could get a blessing. On my place, that is."

"The church generally offers counsel in cases like this. You might have read a lot about exorcisms and the like—there's that famous movie, of course—but most of us, in this diocese anyway, favor a psychological approach."

"That all seems pretty elaborate," said Allen. "I mean, yeah, I'm spooked, but . . . "

The priest smiled. "I understand. I just want you to be aware that, to a large extent, we have to follow protocols. We don't take our sacraments lightly. We always do some amount of, well, I guess you could call it investigation. So it really gets down to questions like, 'What's the environment where these events are taking place?' and 'Are there unresolved conflicts in the home?' and that sort of thing. My advice? It was probably a vivid dream or auditory hallucination. I'm no doctor, but those kinds of experiences are actually quite common. I'd say give it some time. If strange things continue to happen, I'll be more than happy to talk with you again. Please remember, our doors are always open."

Outside the church, Allen felt unmoored. He shook off a chill as he made his way to the bus stop. He was too tired to walk back to Duke's. The 33 Ashbury lumbered up along Eighteenth, then made a left turn, up the curve of upper Market and then into that wide, looping circle of a turn so that it could position itself to continue up Clayton Street. As it did so, the passengers, at least those who cared to look up from their screens, were treated to a sweeping view of the Castro, and then farther out, the downtown skyline, and the bay and Oakland Hills beyond it.

Allen took it in, reminded, once more, of why he loved this city, even if it did seem to be changing by the week lately. *Are you ready?* It was a fair question. Ghost, psychological phantom, or dream, it did haunt him. His career had been eventful and even prosperous in its way, saving him from some soul-killing call of duty in an acreage of corporate cubicles. But at the end of it all, he was still Allen. Still relatively anonymous. The fame he'd once dreamed of had never arrived, and he'd made his peace with that. *I am not alone*, he told himself. *There were times I thought I would be. But I made it. There is that.* He smiled, thinking of Duke, and of his surviving, persistent circle of friends.

The next day, Duke essentially invited himself over, and Allen happily accepted. He drove them back to his place, their conversation falling off as they got closer to Rincon Hill. It was hard to believe, with all of the weekday activity in this part of the city—workers on their lunch break lining up for food trucks, tourists wandering—that a place like Allen's could feel so secluded, but it did, and, to Allen at least, even more so now.

Duke gave him a kind, doubtful but at the same time encouraging look as they got out of the car and walked to Allen's front door. Allen sighed deeply and then let them in. It was still morning, so sunlight from the big east-facing front window made the apartment bright, even welcoming. Still, Allen felt as if they were entering a sanctum of sorts, as if the air, the apartment itself, was taking a read of these new arrivals.

"Mene, mene, tekel upharsin," Allen muttered.

"What?" said Duke.

"The famous writing on the wall," said Allen, not bothering to explain the specific Biblical reference. "Not sure why I said that."

"You can be so obscure sometimes," said Duke.

"Not obscure at all if you . . . ahem . . . read."

"Oh don't *even!* You know I've cracked my share of books," said Duke.

"When is that? Between binge-watching *Real Housewives*?"

Duke gave him an eye roll and did a quick survey of the place. Then they sat on his couch. The apartment looked undisturbed, even peaceful. Duke offered to stay the night but Allen assured him he didn't have to. Even though that's exactly what Allen wanted, he knew it would only be putting off the inevitable. Before Duke left, he gave Allen a hug. "You know where to find us," he said as Allen nodded.

After the door closed, Allen stood looking at his front room. *So what the hell is this telling me?* he thought. Allen had been thinking back to his grade-school days, to the nuns who had taught him, decades ago. All of their assurances that, despite the palpable reality of evil in this world, the good would always triumph. Brenda, or someone, had once instructed him on the distinction between ghosts and demons, the latter being nonhuman entities of pure malevolence. Allen could entertain that ghosts might exist, but he drew the line at nonhuman entities. *The stuff of Lovecraft*, he thought.

A couple of nights later, Duke surprised him, his voice sounding giddy and playful as it came through the intercom. Allen buzzed him in. He toted a big plastic bag with a red *Thank You* on it. Chinese takeout.

"Ah, the food of the gods," said Allen. "And you, young man, are a saint. Especially if there's wine in there too."

Duke smiled and pulled a bottle from another bag.

"And, this isn't just any takeout. It's House of Chen."

"A thousand blessings upon you!" said Allen.

"Well, maybe not so fast with the blessings," said Duke. "They're closing, you know. Did you hear? After about thirty years, I guess."

"Shit," said Allen. "Well, I guess they've earned the right to retire, if that's what it's all about. And don't tell me. I don't want to hear about another local business driven out by greedy land-lords. More importantly, where am I gonna get my lemon chicken now?"

Duke shrugged, as if casting the question to fate. "We'll just have to find another place, and make sure we enjoy the Chen while it lasts."

"And you brought it all the way from the Castro. I must say, the Chens have hired a pretty handsome delivery boy."

"And I do *deliver*," said Duke, giving that last word a comically sexy emphasis.

Allen chuckled. "The food will taste all the better." And it did. They ate at his coffee table, CNN on a very low volume in front of them.

"Anderson Cooper," said Duke. "Talk about a Silver Fox."

"So there's hope for us, is there?"

"For *them*," said Duke. "Don't go lumping yourself in that category just yet. That beard of yours needs some grooming. That, at least, would be a good start."

They sat sipping wine and watched the skyline through the big window, the nearly silent TV and its endless parade of pundits all but unnoticed now. Allen liked the feeling of Duke on his couch, the satisfying sense and weight of another. *His* "another." He had, in the recent weeks, considered himself settled in. He was comfortable. Nothing strange of any kind had happened. He slept well on a regular basis, had his neighborhood routines, such as they were, worked out.

He watched as Duke unwrapped a noisily crinkling cellophane wrapper from a fortune cookie and cracked the tan, crisp pastry in half at the middle. Then he plucked out the little strip of white paper with its red lettering. He read it quietly, then carefully tucked the fortune into a jeans pocket.

"You're not gonna tell me what it says?" Allen asked, playfully.

"Tell me yours," said Duke with a grin. "And I'll tell you mine."

Allen smiled, taking up his cookie, extracting it, and his fortune. He glanced at it, raised an eyebrow, and then read out loud. "'An important investment will pay off.'"

"That sounds hopeful."

"As in, I'd better stop hoping and actually make an investment."

"Maybe you already have," said Duke.

Allen looked slightly puzzled. "I'm not sure what that's supposed to mean. What did yours say?"

Duke cleared his throat and read: "'You will receive a life-changing offer.'" He turned back to watch the effect this had on Allen.

Allen had been staring out at the view. Now he looked at Duke. And then it hit him. *Of course,* he said to himself. And he had a little vision, a fantasy: his front door open, the boxes lined up in the hallway. Then Duke coming in, gently closing the door behind him, and Allen asking, "Is that everything?"

And Duke, smiling broadly, saying "Yeah. It is."

EXIT 17

Tom sat there for a few minutes before he said anything. "We are screwed."

"Seriously?" Steve stared out to the view through the windshield, wanting to believe he really wasn't seeing what he was seeing.

"Yes. Seriously screwed. There's no way we can push ourselves out. I was stupid to even try this. The news said fifty-three was *not* advisable. Hell, they might be shutting it down soon. Drifting snow. Visibility, zilch."

Tom hit the steering wheel, as if that would launch them out of the culvert they'd skidded into.

The two men watched the windshield wipers move the wet snow around in arcs, a rhythmic display that seemed to taunt them.

"That last exit was like, fifteen minutes ago," said Steve.

"Don't remind me," said Tom. "And we haven't seen any cars this whole time. Not even any National Guard patrols. Didn't the news say they'd be out here?" He didn't wait for an answer, and Steve knew it wasn't a question.

"*If* they come," said Steve.

"Thank you, Dr. Obvious."

"Look, don't get short with me." Steve wiped his hand over his face, trying not to hear the plaintive, futile-sounding back-and-forth of the laboring windshield wipers. As if reading his mind, Tom hit the switch to shut them off. The silence seemed thundering.

"So what do you think?" said Tom. "I'm not even going to try and push this thing. We seem to be in here pretty good."

"Yeah," said Steve. "The laws of physics seemed firmly aligned to not be in our favor."

"I think we can wait it out here," said Tom. "At least for a little while. Someone has to come along."

"But *how* long?" asked Steve, his voice rising. "Waiting around doesn't seem like a good option. We've got the car heater but that's only as long as the gas lasts. Three quarters of a tank."

"So you seriously want to try to walk out and get help, in *this*? I don't have to tell you how long the average person lasts in that scenario, do I? Even if you don't get disoriented, that cold will get you quicker than you think." Tom glared at Steve, his anger simmering.

"Okay, we can't both go out. We know that. And I don't think we should just sit here. One of us goes, one of us stays with the car. You ask me, chances are the one that goes will get help quicker. I don't think the National Guard of Ronald Reagan is going to come to our rescue. There's gotta be a farmhouse out over that field there. We're not in Siberia." Steve looked at Tom to see how this registered with him.

"They always say 'Stay with the car.' *Always*. You know this, don't you?"

"If you ask me, that's putting our eggs in one basket," said Steve. "We've gotta maximize our chances here."

Tom looked out into the indistinct blur. "It's just fucked. What happens if you're gone thirty minutes, forty minutes, an hour, two hours? How long do I wait before I try to find you? And if the Guard comes, how do *they* find you?"

"Oh, so I'm elected?" said Steve.

"Oh come on! It's my car!" said Tom.

Steve waved his hands to shut him up. "I get it, I get it, I can go. I was thinking I'd be better at it anyhow, no offense. Those extra donuts have taken their toll."

"Fuck you, Mr. Gym Rat. Okay, fine. Fatty stays with the car," said Tom, sighing. He glanced side to side as if to be sure the weather was as bad as it looked. Then he said, "Hey, I'm sorry man. I guess I'm pissed at myself for getting us into this. If you go out there, that's some serious shit. I know you're in good shape, but I've heard too many stories."

"Yeah. I've thought of the imaginary headlines. Like, 'Fatally Frozen on Fifty-Three: Two Area Men Found in Last Embrace.'"

Tom laughed—and laughed hard—in spite of himself. "That is *not* gonna happen, you sick fuck." They both laughed one last time, then sat in silence.

"So this is the plan?" asked Tom, nervousness rising within him. "Are we really gonna do this?"

Steve nodded.

"Okay," said Tom. "Take a couple candy bars, and that." He pointed to the big industrial-looking flashlight in the backseat. "You'll need it to signal . . . either me, or . . . whoever."

"You think you can signal me back from in here?"

"Yeah, the car's high enough on this side of the culvert that I have enough of a view," said Tom. Steve turned and surveyed it. Mostly swirling snow and not much else, but a light would probably be visible from far off. "Okay, when I get a little ways from the car, I'll test it with you." Tom nodded.

"I got what I need here, for now," said Tom. "I'll keep my eyes out for the Guard. And I got flares. Come to think of it, you should take one of those too."

Steve grabbed one, then patted his down jacket to make sure everything was in place. He gave Tom a look, then opened the door and got out. It didn't take long for him to disappear into the swirling void. Tom didn't like that.

He didn't like it at all.

What bothered Steve most wasn't the first blast of cold that hit him as he closed the car door behind him. No, it was the snow. The instant sense of its constricting depth. Almost up to his knees here, and when he lifted his right foot to begin the ascent from the culvert to the field, he heard the high pitch of its crunch as he took his first step up. The higher the pitch, the colder it was. That's what he'd read somewhere, right? What the hell did it matter? He was already freezing.

Once he was out of the culvert, the wind from across the open plain hit him and nearly took his breath.

He stood for a moment to get his bearings. Down in the culvert below, Tom's car, the light within it, dim as it appeared from here, looked warm and inviting and he thought for a second of abandoning the whole idea and returning to that bit of security it offered, or seemed to. He could easily rationalize his way out of it. *Yeah, you were right, old friend. I'm a crazy fuck to think that would have worked.* And then the two of them smiling, hunkering down to wait.

He felt for the flashlight in his pocket, just to reassure himself that it was still there. He had only taken a few paces away and already the road seemed to disappear into white nothingness, and ahead of him, nothing distinct yet. He tried to find something—a road marker, a utility pole—that he could look for as a return point but nothing seemed distinct or prominent enough. He'd have to rely on his own footprints behind him, but there was no telling how long they'd last.

He sighed, then kept trudging ahead. The snow cover up here was uneven. He tried to avoid the drifts but was mindful to stay in what felt like a straight enough line so that he wouldn't lose his way if he did have to backtrack.

Under the scarf, the inside of his nose had already frozen to an uncomfortable hardness. He remembered that sensation from

Chicago winter mornings when he'd have to walk from his flat off Lincoln to the L station, then stand on the platform to wait like all the other poor huddled masses.

After what felt like twenty minutes or so, he did a careful 360-degree turn on his feet to take stock of where he was, which was, for all intents and purposes, the middle of a cold white void. He concentrated his gaze on the indistinct view ahead. He thought he could make out a foggy-looking light in the distance, but he wasn't sure. Maybe it was some sort of optical illusion. He'd heard that mountain climbers and people in other extreme, wilderness-related situations sometimes see things that aren't there. In the case of the climbers, they'd reportedly seen images of themselves, doppelgangers, climbing alongside them. The thought creeped him out.

If that fucking happens here . . . he said to himself. And then he wondered if his piss and shit would freeze at this temperature.

Minutes later, he was sure he could discern the outline of structure. A barn, maybe? Some outbuilding? If he was lucky, a house. Even an empty house would still have a phone, and he guessed he'd be forgiven for breaking and entering, considering the circumstances.

But he was getting ahead of himself.

Well shit, you were right, it was worth it. Tom was in his head now.

You see? He replied to Tom. *Don't doubt me. I'm a native Midwesterner. We just have a sense for these things.* In his mind's eye, Steve saw Tom sitting in the warm car, rolling his eyes at this. *Just make it quick, man, okay? We've got better things to do. I owe you a beer at the next town.*

An Irish coffee would be better, Steve thought. He saw Tom nod in silent assent, as if to say, *You've earned one, my friend.*

The wind had picked up a bit and Tom felt it cutting, razor-like, at the still-exposed skin between the end of his scarf and the top of his hood. It even seemed to work its way a bit inside the hood, as if to remind him of its relentlessness. He squinted ahead and, yes, it was definitely a building, still a hike away but ahead of him now. He picked up his pace, and the depth of the snow seemed to rise, as if to meet his new energy with a determination to thwart him.

Almost there, bro. He wasn't sure if he liked Tom's voice in his head or not. But it did seem to help.

This is harder than I thought, Steve admitted.

I gotta hand it to you. It didn't take you long to find something. I'd call that progress, right?

Steve nodded in silent agreement, intent now on studying the shape that was emerging into clarity as he approached. Rectangular. A wall of corrugated steel. Definitely not a house, but something. He felt a metallic chill, as if his body needed to register the matter-of-fact reality in front of him.

He was up against the wall of it now. About thirty-five feet long, eight or nine feet up. Some kind of barn or garage, maybe full of farm equipment. He circled around it to the right and saw the door and an unlit garage light just above it. The door was solidly locked. No signs or indication of any kind about what might be inside. No HAZMAT placards either, which would be required on a building containing fertilizer or pest-control chemicals. So there might be vehicles in there. But what he needed now, most immediately, was warmth, or at least the promise of it.

As he turned the next corner, he saw just what he wanted to see—another building, maybe fifty paces beyond this one, but definitely the shape of railings around a porch and a gabled roof over two stories. No lights, but most definitely a house. He felt his heart lift and he quickened his pace, at least as much as the snow would let him.

He started to sweat a little under his heavy coverage, and tried to remember if that was a good thing or a bad thing. He could rest when he got to the house; even a porch would work, just enough of a windbreak.

We forgot to test it. Well, technically, you forgot to test it. Tom was in his head again.

Test what? Steve asked.

The flashlight. Remember? I flashed from the car but you probably didn't see it because you were walking away from me.

Steve cursed at himself. He was angry that he'd screwed up and that, as a result, Tom now had one on him. Steve was the one who'd missed a key, critical element of their plan.

Relax, man. Sorry. I'm not gonna ride you about it. Just see what you can find out and we'll go from there. Deal?

"Deal," said Steve, aloud. Then he realized he was talking to a voice inside of his head. For all he knew, Tom was singing along to the radio in the car, thinking of anything other than Steve.

He roomed with Tom in the dorm back at Belmont College. They'd lived together for three years before Tom moved off campus. Steve had opted to stay on at the honors dorm, earning a room of his own during his senior year. It had been a bleak and lonely one too. The year before, Steve had come out to Tom. This was the mid '70s, in the Midwest, and there was no guarantee that Tom would take it well, but to Steve's relief, he did. But he'd always wondered. Was that the reason Tom moved out of the dorm the next year?

He'd once overheard Tom, deride the "bloody poofters" to a UK friend who was visiting that semester as they watched a popular New Wave band on Tom's tiny black-and-white TV. Some British music show that the local PBS station sometimes ran. When Steve had walked in on the tail of that comment, Tom looked instantly sheepish. Then he made some unrelated joke and the three of them laughed it off.

No, Tom's a good guy. He said to himself as he walked. If he ever did have less-than-admirable, less-than-enlightened ideas about gays, he must have moved beyond all that by now, right? It was almost ten years ago.

He found himself standing in front of the house. His heart sank when he saw thick boards nailed to the windows on the ground floor. A huge, Armageddon-proof-looking padlock had been put in place to secure the front door. And not that he expected to see any, but there were no lights, no signs of habitation of any kind, visible through the windows of the second floor.

Well that, said Tom's voice, *is decidedly not promising.*

"Okay, let's get something straight," said Steve. "First of all, I don't appreciate your cynicism and your insistence on providing your little running commentary on all this. You were right, OKAY? I should have stayed in the fucking car! Can you just do me a favor and shut up . . . unless you have something instructive to add?"

You realize you're talking to yourself, don't you? Actually, you're sort of shouting. Sorry. Does that count as 'instructive'? Oh, also, I think you meant 'constructive.'

Steve tried to calm himself, still watching the house. Well, this was enough. He'd come, he'd seen, and he had definitely not conquered. It was time to walk back to the car.

Don't worry buddy, all is forgiven. Just get the hell back here.

Steve turned and walked back to the garage structure. He could see remnants of his footprints, but already they'd started to fade. He guessed any other tracks he'd made on his way out had been even more erased, at this point. But there were enough by the garage for him to launch his way back toward where he was sure Tom and the car were waiting.

It wasn't that long ago, and it wasn't that far. Ten minutes or so and I'll be back. Yeah, Tom will give me shit, but hell, at least we'll have the satisfaction of knowing we tried. No more need for adventure. And maybe, by then, Tom will have another idea, or maybe he'll have flagged someone down.

Steve realized he was feeling hungry, so he dug out one of the candy bars. It was in a shiny, bright red wrapper. Something called *Big Bonanza.*

Where the hell did he get this? Well, whatever, it's lunch now. And I guess it's a good sign I'm hungry.

The cold had rendered the chocolate bar rock hard, and Steve felt he might chip a tooth biting into it, but he managed to break off a chewable piece, and from then on, eating it was easier. The taste of the chocolate and the nuts was sheer heaven. It didn't take him long to devour it. He felt satisfied once he was done.

He kept on walking. He looked at his watch. It had been about twelve minutes since he'd left the abandoned structures. *Had it really taken him that long to get to them in the first place?* Peering ahead, the snow as thick as ever, maybe even thicker, Steve saw no sign of any road or car. But he kept on.

How you doin' there, buddy?

Steve was relieved to hear Tom's voice, imagined or not. *Can't complain, he said. Just trudging along. Should be back to you soon.*

Roger that.

And now Steve was remembering a party they'd had in their dorm room, during their second year. Tom had mixed a huge batch of margaritas and had also secured a keg. It was a kind of winter semester blowout, something they put together "just because" as Tom had said. At least a dozen people crammed into their room, getting progressively drunker, and hornier.

Steve remembered Tom sort of playing at making out with—what was her name, Janice? A woman from the women's floor upstairs.

He caught Tom's eye across the room at one point. People had mostly wandered out and the party was quieting. A small assortment of amorous couples had claimed chairs or beds around the room. At this point, they'd moved from kissing to quiet, hushed conversation. No doubt plans were afoot for scattered rendezvous elsewhere.

But Tom's look had been . . . different. At the time, Steve thought it was a Hey-Buddy-I'm-Gonna-Need-the-Room Look. It had happened before. Back then, Tom had been in very good shape, and he'd been prolific in the love department. But there was something in his smile, Steve now realized, something almost leering. Like Tom was needling him, teasing Steve for being so alien to the world of good old-fashioned heterosexuality.

"It's fucking my room too!" he said out loud.

Tom chimed in, as if Steve's outburst had pulled him away from some other task. *What was that buddy? You talking to yourself again?*

Steve felt instantly sobered, if that was the word.

Christ, how long has it been now? At least I'm not shivering. In fact, all this fucking walking is making me warm as fuck. With that, he unzipped his down jacket and loosened the scarf. The cold air felt refreshing as it moved in around him, or least, that's what it felt like it was doing.

Much better, he thought. *But I'd better keep moving.*

Steve had tried to date when he was at Belmont, but back in those days, that meant making the hour-or-so drive to Detroit to hit up the bars he'd heard about. There were a couple he'd relied on, and he'd even had a few one-night hookups, but those had been few and far between. There were guys from U of M, a lot of them, and he'd spent some of those nights in Ann Arbor.

One night Tom found a friend with a car and they'd taken Steve and a few other guys from campus, guys that Tom knew from his hunting club, and they'd hit up some of the straight bars in Ann Arbor. Steve had resigned himself to a monkish night of romance-free observation and the need to deflect questions from the other guys about which women he found attractive.

But one of the men in Tom's group, a tall blond who seemed to have a decidedly quieter cast than the rest of them, but with a halting and appealingly sarcastic vein of humor, caught his eye. Or, he should say, they'd caught each other's eyes. This guy— Edward, maybe?—had been driving. He'd been the one who'd actually secured the car; Tom had only recruited the others to come along. Steve kept looking up to see Ed's eyes locking with his in the rearview mirror. The first time was a fluke. The second time was not. By the third time, they both knew.

Even now, nearly ten years later, Steve could see Ed's face and feel a bit of the exhilaration he'd felt when he'd talked with Ed casually, but they had both been weirdly careful to not come out and say anything to each other. And, they'd gotten quite drunk. Almost all of them had. Surprisingly, it was Tom who ended up as the group's designated driver. Steve and Ed ended up sitting next to each other in the back seat for the somewhat long ride home. But Steve, for once, had not minded the distance and the time required for them to get back to campus. As the nondescript landscape rolled by outside, he'd been wired, tuned in to every nuance, every pulse of activity and movement and feeling that seemed coiled up in the body of Ed, who was now by his side. Yes, their legs had touched. First, tentatively, and then definitively.

All of this had remained firmly within the zone of the subtle until, at some point, the guys in that backseat became drowsy, and Steve found his head on Ed's shoulder. Somewhere along the line he'd been aware, he thought, of a ripple of unease in the car. Ed stiffened beside him, and then gently nudged him away. Steve had drifted in and out of sleep to the sound of the music from the car's tape deck . . . those bulky eight-tracks that would interrupt longer songs for the track switch . . . giving the music a kind of ethereal quality.

The next day, in the dorm cafeteria, Steve saw Tom with some of his friends from the night before. Ed was not among them. Some of them glanced his way, smiling sarcastically. He saw one of them lean in toward the group, make a comment that he could not hear, and the group laughed loudly. *That* he could hear.

Steve was surprised at how vividly these memories were coming back. He hadn't thought about that episode with Tom in years, and now he was all but reliving it. Something brought him back to the present. He was finding it difficult to walk and keep his balance.

Fucking snow, he said, as he lifted one foot, then the next. A part of him really wanted to rest. He looked down at his feet and realized that his coat was gone. It must have somehow worked loose after he'd unzipped it a while back. Not having it actually made him feel more comfortable and less overheated. Still, it had been an expensive coat. He turned to look for it, thinking he'd seen it lying on top of the snow a few yards back, but there was nothing but snow, and his fading tracks. And as soon as he registered that there was nothing there, he forgot why he'd looked in the first place, and he turned back to the landscape ahead of him and continued his slow progress toward . . .

Toward what? he asked himself. *Where exactly am I going?*

So he stopped. All around him, a featureless expanse. He wondered if campus was close, thinking it was Belmont he'd been heading toward. He did not recognize this place.

Well, snow will do that. That's the magic of it. It comes down and covers everything and the world is white, clean, and pure. Pure. He repeated the word to himself, liking the sound of it. *Pure.*

Am I pure? Am I without sin? Oh no. How I have sinned. God forgive me. I have been impure in thought. And maybe in deed too. God, merciful God, please forgive me . . .

He saw something ahead. It took him a while to focus. Something slightly darker than the surrounding background of snow, something nearly distinct, something that seemed to be taking shape as he got ever so slowly closer. The prospect of discovery briefly energized him and propelled him forward with renewed purpose.

It's a shape, all right, he told himself. *Not a building . . . maybe a tree? An animal. No, it's a person. Yes, a person . . . well, two of them. Two people moving toward him.*

He raised a hand to wave, not realizing that no one at that distance, in these conditions, would likely see it. Steadily they drew closer together, Steve and these newcomers.

In another minute, they were in front of him. The three stopped to regard each other. It was Tom. And coming up behind Tom, the other person, who had been lagging, drew near. He too stood now in front of Steve, who was alternately amazed and annoyed to see this man wearing the coat he'd lost. The man looked alarmingly familiar. He had Steve's coat, Steve's clothes, Steve's hair, and Steve's face.

Before Steve could summon the will to put into speech any of the many questions coursing through his consciousness, Tom spoke.

Hey Buddy, he said, smiling hugely, as if he'd just won the lottery. *I got someone here I want you to meet.*

THE PLOT

The landscaper heard screams from grave 2022. At least he thought he did. He turned off the weed whacker and stopped to listen in late morning silence. Two gray squirrels scampered in an old oak thirty yards away.

He walked over to 2022. The Garrison grave. They'd buried the kid the other day. A car crash. Terrible. Huge funeral. He heard the mother had epically lost it. Who could blame her?

He bent down. He thought about shouting over the grave but felt stupid for thinking it. He could just hear Adams, the general manager, saying, "Muzzy, you're fucking nuts." *Fuckin' Adams.* Sometimes he hated him. *Smug jackass.* It was bad enough that Adams ribbed him for his out-of-date equipment, like the cord of the whacker. *Hey, it still works*, Muzzy thought. *Better than the cheap shit they make now.* But Mike Muzzachowski had been doing landscaping here for nine years now, and Adams helped keep his business solidly in the black. *If times were better*, he thought, *I'd lose Adams and his "Creepy Acres."*

The weed whacker, he thought. *Maybe if I turn it on again . . .* well, maybe the kid would hear that. He stopped himself. *This is fucking crazy.* But he turned it back on, revved it a little around the plot's edges—the new marker wasn't there yet, but the sod over the dig was plain as day. He revved, then crouched down to listen.

This time he heard something, muffled and far down, but something. The grave was still new. It hadn't settled. Before he knew it, he was running, then banging at the door of the cemetery office, the sound ringing hollow inside. He ran to the window around the corner. Sure enough, there was Adams, at his desk, black headphone buds in each ear. Muzzy pounded. Then he thought, *Call him!* But when he tapped his pocket, his phone wasn't there. Could have fallen out on the grounds. Could be anywhere. He searched for it, then saw something off about 2022. Some old bum sleeping. But he looked clean. And something else, really weird . . . tufts of grass being kicked up violently beside the sleeper. It was the weed whacker. He must have dropped it to the ground and somehow it was still going. It blazed blindly in manic circles. Then he got closer. Saw the guy's jeans. The shirt. Both the same as his. Then the same beard. The same face. And a wispy, thin blue smoke he recognized as what comes from electrical burning, rising slowly from the clothes.

PIERCE AND HAWTHORNE

FRANKLIN PIERCE, DECADES BEFORE his phenomenal failure as the fourteenth US President and the personal tragedies that haunted him to his end, dozed in half-sleep as the carriage carrying him to his last year at Bowdoin College passed the deep, wraith-filled shadows of the Maine woods. The ride to Brunswick usually lulled him, but as he got closer to campus and the hills gave way to the flat, pine-covered plains along the road, he grew more alert. Bowdoin had always meant a kind of freedom for him, but now it meant the end of his old life and the start of a new one. He regarded the passing scenery; despite the vibrant fall colors, the afternoon light seemed plaintive. It was the time for last things.

He hadn't read any of the Cicero, Virgil, or Sallust he'd brought with him for the trip; he preferred thinking of the nights when he and his friends, Nathaniel Hawthorne and Zenas Caldwell, would sneak off to the tavern. On cool nights, they made their way through the woods, glimpsing the Androscoggin River through the trees, and anticipating the fire waiting for them at the tavern.

It would all end soon enough. He and Caldwell would leave Hawthorne behind and join the world. Thinking of Caldwell, who always kidded him about his studies, he decided to read his Cicero after all, and turned to his essay on the virtues of growing old. He had read the words so many times before, had struggled first with the Latin, but now found himself approaching a sense of what the great man had said. He wanted to believe that these were words he would hearken back to one day, far off in his future, but now he wondered about the restlessness of youth, and when, if ever, it might subside. Hawthorne, in particular, had made Pierce feel that there was so much that was good in them in these days, and Pierce hated to think of the goodbyes they'd share at the end of the year. Too much seemed final.

After he'd established himself in his bare room in Maine Hall—the new wood smelling fresh after the rebuilding from last year's fire—he sought out Hawthorne in the rush of the new students. Just as he approached, Hawthorne turned to greet him with typical retreat and quietness. His dark eyes were intense. "Nate," said Pierce, shaking his hand with vigor. "I see one more year has changed you, brightened you. It's good to see you again, my friend." Hawthorne reddened a bit as he beheld his friend's face once more. "Frank," he said. "More ready for the tavern, I suspect, than for the old books that await us here." They stood for a moment smiling and taking each other in after their absence; Pierce felt as if he had arrived home.

As they were talking they heard the cries of Uncle Trench, pushing his wheelbarrow from which he sold his gingerbread and, when he was able, root beer. "Plain and sugared! Plain and sugared!" he called out. His voice, slight and weathered, still managed to carry over the loud talk, shouts and bursts of laughter from the students renewing their acquaintances all around the square. As soon as they heard Trench's familiar voice they paused in their conversations, dug coins from their pockets, and began to crowd around the old man. "Ah, our venerable Uncle Trench," said Pierce, nudging Hawthorne. "I do believe his wheelbarrow has become permanently attached to his hands." Hawthorne laughed with him as they approached the old man. "Come, let's see what he has," said Pierce, reaching into his own pocket and stopping Hawthorne from doing the same.

They joined the group around Trench. "Come now, lads, come now," said the salesman, warming to his craft. "Plain and sugared! Plain and sugared!"

"Any root beer, Uncle Trench?" called out a student.

"None, my lads, none today," to which the students answered with a chorus of groans. Then they took up a chant, playfully mimicking him. "Plain and sugared! Plain and sugared!" Trench took their coins and doled out the gingerbread, soon running out of the favorite sugared ones. He announced this hesitantly, provoking a new wave of groans and jeers.

Hawthorne and Pierce retreated to a spot near the lumber pile next to Maine Hall and unwrapped their gingerbread from its paper, eating it quickly, in silence. "Were you thinking, my friend," said Hawthorne, searching his outspread wrapper for crumbs, "that we should inaugurate this new year with a visit to the tavern tonight? Caldwell might even dare to go this time."

"I have a much better idea than that, Nate."

Hawthorne waited, curious and smiling as Pierce readied to reveal his new plan.

"Let's go, tonight, to see the Sibyl. We'll bring our coin and have her read our futures for us. What better way to start the new year here?" Pierce saw what he thought was a shade of doubt darkening Hawthorne's face. He discounted it, and continued, "We shall find what the fates have in store for us." He smiled and reached over to touch the younger man's shoulder. "Are you with me, Nate?"

"Ah, the black arts," said Hawthorne. "President Allen would surely frown upon his students embarking on such a pilgrimage." He paused dramatically, regarding Pierce with a face of mock seriousness. Suddenly he broke into laughter, "For that reason, then, I am with you!" Pierce joined him in his laugh, relieved to see that his friend had softened in the time since he'd last seen him, and that the doubt he thought he'd seen had been imagined. "Yes, I will go with you, Frank."

The two parted to finish the business of settling into their respective houses. Later that day they met up, as agreed, at the Paradise spring in the forest that surrounded the campus. There were clumps of students here and there, some smoking clandestine cigars, enjoying a last respite before their studies were to begin.

Pierce entered this enclave and saw Hawthorne's shadowy form soon enough, and the two of them set off toward the shack, the other boys, seeing their direction, looked away quickly so as not to curse their fortune, whatever it might be. The Sibyl had long been warning them of the dark powers of thought and the evil eye.

Hawthorne followed Pierce as they negotiated the old path. As they approached her shack, Pierce caught a glimpse, through the trees, of the last of the late light on the waters of the river. Its presence permeated their life on the campus, and in these woods. When they swam at the Paradise spring once the weather turned at the end of the year, when they played cards underneath the pines, the river was there, its voice soothing them, carrying them on.

"What will she say, do you think?" said Pierce to Hawthorne as they worked their way through the foliage.

"What she says to all of us, of course: Wealth in your future. Beautiful women. Good fortune. She knows enough not to spoil her well. She knows where her coin comes from."

"Still," said Pierce, "I sometimes feel a touch of fear when I think of her, and of all that she knows."

"Then you haven't attended well to Professor Cleaveland's lectures. There is nothing sure or solid in the life of our world but the rocks we walk on, the air we breathe," said Hawthorne. "Aren't these the only things we know for sure? The only things worth knowing? Who can claim to lay hold the life of the spirit or the mind of God?"

"You do not sound like yourself, Nate," said Pierce. "I had thought that you were much more willing to accept the reality of the spirit world. Are you not the one, after all, who searches the heavens for signs of the divine? How are we to know then, if we are to be saved? How shall we read our fates if we cannot read them in the book of nature? Isn't that how our Lord makes his will known to us?"

He listened in amusement to Hawthorne's silence behind him. "You should return to your Cicero, Frank," said his friend finally. "Your skills as a debater have suffered in your summer absence from this place." Pierce's laughter echoed in the trees. Hawthorne watched Pierce's solid figure ahead of him, truly glad to be in his friend's company once more.

They reached the Sibyl's shack, which they still, even after coming here over the years, regarded with a hushed awe. The light seemed to attain a new quality, not so much darker, but fuller, somehow, heavier. The long, leaning structure of her dwelling looked to be of the trees and the loam around it, surrounded by pine, calla, pogonia, and calapogon. It seemed almost precarious, as if it had grown up accidentally, the product of some wayward seed, at this elevated perch alongside the swift-running river. Pierce took the lead, positioning himself carefully before the shack's window-less front door. He knocked in the manner that all who visited from Bowdoin had learned—three quick knocks, a pause, and two more. They waited, and then heard the old woman's cracked voice from within. "What bring you?"

Pierce looked at Hawthorne and smiled as he intoned the greeting required from the Sibyl. "We have coin for the Seer. We've come to hear our fortunes."

"Come in then," she said, sounding as if she'd grown weary of her own formalities.

They opened the door and were greeted by the rich, pungent odor of the Sibyl's pipe tobacco, which she smoked incessantly. Despite her reputation, the fanciful descriptions of her as a hag that were passed down from student to student, the Sibyl was actually quite neat in appearance. She dressed in layers of shawl that invari-ably looked clean and well-kept. Her hair was white, but she wore it pulled back into a tight, neatly arranged bun. Only her wrinkled skin betrayed the roughness of her years, but she bore herself with a quiet dignity that never failed to win the respect of her visitors.

"Come in," she said, waving them closer. "Come near the light of this fire and I will read the book of your fates, lads. Do pay me first, I ask." They dropped the coins into her outstretched hands, and she looked at them briefly before placing them in a bag at her side. "Sit before me, lads, and I will look at you."

She held her hand out to Hawthorne first, and he obliged by meeting it with his own, She took it silently and looked at it. Then she cast tea leaves, and peered into the small bowl. "You, my son," she said. "The wheel turns toward you with its favor, and its favor is wealth. There is, also, another greatness in you. You are a blessed fair one," she said to him with a ragged smile. Hawthorne blushed crimson at her words and thanked the Sibyl humbly.

She turned her gaze upon Pierce. "And you," she said, "I remember you. You are the one they call 'Handsome Frank'?"

Hawthorne watched with amused amazement. He had not suspected that his friend Pierce had visited the Sibyl as much as he apparently had. Pierce looked at him, daring a conspiratorial smile, but the Sibyl did not notice this.

"Ah," she said, holding his hand and peering into it. "For you, I think, I shall need the cards." Pierce and Hawthorne exchanged hurried, nervous glances. Pierce began to reach for more coins but she stopped him. "Not now, lad. Not now. I must read."

She retrieved her stack of aged Tarot cards, their colored inks long faded beyond their original vibrancy. She had Pierce touch the deck, then laid them out before him. With the first card she drew, she uttered a little cry.

"No, no, it is just as I'd felt," she said. "I am afraid it is just as I felt." She beckoned Pierce closer and held up the card for him. It was "The Tower," which pictured a high structure on a precipice, struck by lightning and in flames as two figures fell from it, one of them crowned. She rested her hand against the young man's cheek. Hawthorne watched the aged hand resting there, for that one moment, almost as if she wanted to impart to Pierce whatever power she had, whatever could defend him from his fate. She regarded him, almost tearfully. "Ruin," she said. "Misery. I have dreamed of this card, dear Handsome Frank. I had hoped it would not return to me, but it has. Go now and I will work for you to avoid this ruin. I will burn an offering, but you must go now, my fair one. Say nothing of this. When you think of it, rub your hands in earth and walk backwards in a circle three times. Go now, with your friend, and I will work for you to be lifted of this darkness."

Hawthorne rose quickly and climbed up through the Sibyl's door and Pierce followed. He dared not look back. They walked down to the main path and headed to Maine Hall in silence, saying nothing along the way. Hawthorne could not remember ever hearing of the Sibyl delivering such a pronouncement. He watched Pierce as his friend walked silently before him in the now darkening woods. It seemed to him that the moon had come alive in the sky then, that the trees themselves were conversing in their gentle rustles, and that the whole of nature, all around them, knew of the terrible line the young men had traveled beyond and from which they could never return.

While Hawthorne waited in the distance, separated from him by the thick of the trees, Pierce stopped in a small clearing to do as the Sibyl had instructed. He stooped and dug into the rich soil under the thicket of leaves and pine needles. It came up thick and damp in his hands, and he rubbed them in it vigorously, breathing in its aroma. Then he stood, arms outstretched, and walked the backwards circles. He wondered what she had seen in him, what she had hoped he could step away from and turn into a better course of time. He stopped to steady himself after completing the circles.

In the distance, somewhere in the thick of the trees, Pierce heard a movement and stood in the darkening light trying to see. "It can't be Hawthorne," he thought. "He's standing on the other side." Pierce edged forward toward the site of the noise but all was dead silence now. Gradually he became aware of a form standing off in the shadows, the tall figure of a man. He was clear in his outline but Pierce could not make out a face, and in that instant he felt he recognized it as human, he sensed that it too, had been regarding him and was just as doubtful about what it was seeing. Pierce thought he saw it start, and that its hand had moved up toward its face. He stood frozen, unable to stop staring. Then he heard Hawthorne call out to him. The form was still there. He backed away from it, and in the brief time that it took to leave the little clearing and return to Hawthorne, he felt the indescribable tug and weight of being watched from afar.

He rejoined Hawthorne and they continued their walk back to campus in silence. Hawthorne thought that the wind had come up around them colder now. He watched his friend Pierce, ahead of him, and it was as if his shadow had been marked, painted over with the dark shadings of a fate predestined.

At the door of the hall, before they ascended to their rooms, the two friends stood regarding each other in the evening light. Pierce saw a mournful sadness, and questioning, in Hawthorne's eyes and he had to turn away. He could not answer to what troubled Hawthorne because it troubled him, too, with equal mystery, and speaking of it might somehow give it more power than it already had. When he was alone in his room, Pierce lay on his bed without removing his coat. He remembered the long, wordless return journey from the Sibyl. He thought again of the spell he had tried to cast, the hope of discarding whatever it was that burdened his future. He thought of what had watched him from the shadows. Even as he lay in his bed that night, he thought he could hear the sound of the Androscoggin, its waters tentative against its banks, as if to spare the world the flow of time. This is what whispered to him, and he dreaded the sound now, even as it followed him and lifted him into sleep.

ROOM 410

Who ever strives with all his power, We are allowed to save.
    The Angels, *Faust, Part II.*

Hyrum Schmidt spread his arms wide, straight, and stiff like a
scarecrow as the tailor, Mr. Hu, a pleasant and talkative Chinese
man, busily chalked the sleeves, the back, the sides, and the legs of
the unfitted suit he had donned—its dark blue fabric draped over
Schmidt's hands and bunched at his feet.

"You are a solid man, Mr. Schmidt," said the tailor, his English
polished and precise. "You work hard. I can tell."

Schmidt liked Mr. Hu's chatter. In fact, he found it somewhat
pleasant, even soothing, but he preferred to talk as little as possible,
and he knew that Mr. Hu was used to his manner, his taciturnity.
Perhaps Mr. Hu sensed that Schmidt also, a child of immigrants,
was careful about his transactions. It was a force of habit, and Mr.
Hu could see in Mr. Schmidt, the banker, the mark of habit.

"A new hat for you today, too?" inquired Mr. Hu, and seeing
Schmidt nod, Hu reached up to measure his head. Schmidt felt the
soft cloth of the old yellow tape measure as Mr. Hu wrapped it
around his balding pate. "Must make sure," said Mr. Hu, laughing
genially. "So long since your last hat. Maybe you are smarter now,
eh?" He tapped his own forehead, laughing a bit too loud at his

own joke. Yes, Mr. Hu thought, the habit of silence. Mr. Hu knew that such a thing comes from life. It is something one puts upon oneself, like a carefully selected suit. Best not to intrude upon it.

"You are very thorough, Mr. Hu. I appreciate that," said Schmidt, smiling and stepping down from the block and away from the mirrors. It was true that he liked Mr. Hu's demeanor, and he always felt better in his store. It had the quietness of a library, or a secluded lounge. Schmidt hadn't treated himself to the luxury of a suit in a long time, though he'd seen Mr. Hu often enough for alterations and the like. After years of making things stretch, Schmidt felt entitled to an indulgence. In the small fitting room, the return to his old and somewhat worn brown suit seemed to confirm his decision. Schmidt felt a small shading of pleasure, like a comforting breeze, and what startled him about it was the realization that this simple peacefulness struck him as something unfamiliar, a thing long gone and now suddenly returned, as if to remind him of the larger currents of life.

Mr. Hu had called him a "solid man." Schmidt laughed to himself at the phrase. Perhaps it was a not unkind way of remarking on his somewhat stocky build, his advancing middle age. *Ein bisschen dick*, thought Schmidt as he regarded himself in the mirror one last time before departing. Perhaps a little fat, but not much.

Schmidt had been efficient with his time today, so he could afford the diversion of a small stroll as he made his way back to the bank. He angled up First Street for the view of the Sound, which he favored. Gray sky and water. The big dark ships looking majestic in the distance. It felt like a big cozy kitchen to Schmidt, the big sink of the nautical world coming home to roost at the edge of the city. Schmidt still could not acquaint himself with the size of America. At night he dreamed of the continent that he had seen as he rode West. The memory of the train's gentle motion lulled him even now, as if he were still carried upon it, as if he were still being floated, heavenly, across the sleeping night of the country, dotted with lights in its far-off fields and farms. Lights of far-off houses and towns like stars in the vast night sky. By day, the space of the land, the cities, and the crowds of people sometime made him stop and wonder. But he was growing used to city life now.

As he stood on the corner of Hennepin and Second Street, waiting for the signal to cross, he scanned the headlines of *The Intelligencer* and the other papers offered for sale at the stand there.

Byrd Announces Plan for South Pole Flight.

Coolidge Will Not Run—"I had no idea," says First Lady.

Penicillin's Promise Great.

There seemed to be a great optimism in the world. As he looked back at the last several years, the world had been fizzling with a kind of delight, as if it had shaken off the Great War at last. But Schmidt felt a heaviness tugging at him. Or perhaps, a better description, an emptiness. Schmidt was indeed a creature of habit. Punctual, predictable, regimented—it was woven into his fabric tightly. Each day he walked to his office at Columbia Bank and each day he walked back, the tiny minute hand of his Elgin watch making its rapid circuit. Curiously, it was the one thing Schmidt owned that reminded him of home.

But home, now, was his spacious apartment in the Hotel Pierce. He was lucky that it afforded him a view of the Sound. It was there that he climbed, at the end of this and every other day, up the wide creaking stairs to his silent rooms. It was there his canvas awaited him. He had taken to painting—his easel and unfinished canvas draped in a sheet in the corner by the large windows. That evening after returning home from the bank and having his small supper, Schmidt removed the canvas from its corner and carefully took the sheet off, revealing a rectangular surface on which he had traced out his view of the city. Schmidt was surprised with his own skill as a draftsman, but the painting itself had been more challenging. It had taken him a long time to acquaint himself with the texture and feel of the thick oils as he laid them on. But now his city was taking shape.

His wife Elizabeth, dead these many years, watched him from her corner for a long time before she spoke. *Such shapes Hyrum, such colors. Is this truly the way the world looks now?*

I forget that you have not seen it in so long, my dear, but yes. So much is different here. Not just a different time, but a different place. It is so strange, I find, to live so near the water, to feel it in the air when you breathe. In Minnesota, our air was different. The light was different. And of course, this is the city.

Schmidt worked a while as she watched. He wondered what she thought of the sight of the thin brush in his heavy hand. He could feel her appraising the canvas—it was the only way she had, now, of knowing the world. *My dear Elizabeth, you would not believe the crowds. The people. Even now, after all this time here, I still find myself awed by them. We never had such a thing there, never such a press. The space here is so different. We are both, I think, within a new life.*

Schmidt was tempted to turn to look at her, but he had learned that he could not, that she would only speak to him and that he could feel her there but that this had to be enough. He never knew how long she would remain. Today, she seemed uncharacteristically restless.

It took me a while to find you, after the storm, she said. She had, of course, told him this before, but she always said it. It was part of her way of coming back to him, and, he feared, it would be part of her finally leaving him again. He remembered the first time all too well. That hot, sweltering day in Muldoon, the heaviness of the spring storm coming, the dank, hot swelter that carried all the foreboding of the dramatic. They had come to know what such days meant. He had told her, before driving into town, to keep close to the cellar if the wind came, to be on the lookout for the dark, quilted clouds. Still, it had seemed to the town as if the tornado had come from a blank sky, as if it had issued ex nihilo. Schmidt painted on, but he knew that she had left. In the silence, he continued to paint the dark buildings at the edge of the water.

Schmidt had taken to courting one of the tellers in his bank. She was young, very young, perhaps half his age, but she smiled kindly upon him, or so he fancied, and he soon found himself courting her in his way. They walked through the park at midday. Though she never asked him, he talked often of life in Minnesota.

"Oh, you're a funny one, Hyrum," she cooed. "A real funny one!" This remark inevitably followed when he offered her some small tenderness, like a flower or a wrapped chocolate from the corner confectioner.

Though she was only what he liked to think of as commonly pretty, Schmidt found himself taken with Claire O'Connor. She had, he thought, the heart to listen to him. She had asked about his family, if he indeed still had a family back East, and Schmidt was hesitant to answer. He offered generalities and only hinted that there was no one left. He could not find it within himself to paint for her the picture of what had happened. Even as he remembered it, he felt the chill of the sudden advancing front that had come across his life that day.

As they sat on the park bench, she buzzed happily, humming a tune as the two of them ate sandwiches from a brown paper bag and the city bustled all around them. "Hyrum, do you know that song, 'Black Bottom?' Oh, I can't get it out of my head. Let's see, how does it go?" She hummed the gay tune for him, her eyes lit up, and his enchanted. Still, even in moments like this, he ached to tell her that the world had shadows, and that these could come down, and come down hard.

The face of his wife, Elizabeth, and their young daughter, Katherine, the sight of his house in the fields of Minnesota, the play of the light upon the trees in his yard . . . all these things existed in his memory. For on April 12 of 1928, Muldoon, Minnesota, after sweltering through a day in which time itself seemed to be suspended, had been hit with the black wall of a deadly tornado. By the time Schmidt had been able to leave the safety of the marble-fronted bank where he worked (one of the few structures in Muldoon to survive the storm), the great funnel cloud was still lumbering across the open fields away from the town. He watched it through the windscreen as the motor sputtered, and he sped toward home, or what had been his home. The funnel cloud now looked bouyant, almost benign as it twirled slowly off toward its own oblivion. With it went Schmidt's life. His wife, his daughter, his home—swept away in the violence of a spring storm.

Months later, Schmidt, like many who had lived in the town all their lives, moved away. He chose to venture west, where a cousin had promised him a job in one of the city's oldest financial institutions. Schmidt had not been sure if he was ready for the change, and the prospect of being in a large city frightened him. He could not imagine that fate would find him there, lost in the crowds of commerce and progress. What he had not counted on was the toll of the loneliness and routine. His cousin's family had been receptive at first, and sympathetic, but it soon became clear that Schmidt would have to find his own way. And in truth, he simply did not have much in common with these distant offshoots of his family.

Later that day, Mr. Harper, the bank president, approached Schmidt. "Mr. Schmidt, can I see you for a moment, please?" Schmidt followed him into his office and closed the door behind him as he took a seat in front of Mr. Harper's desk. The chair felt inviting and comfortable, but Schmidt had a bad feeling.

"Mr. Schmidt, what you do with your personal time is none of my business, but when you spend any part of that time with another employee of this bank, particularly when it is with one as pretty as Miss O'Connor, it does become my business. I certainly do not enjoy having to tell you this, Mr. Schmidt, but I must ask you—I must tell you—that you are not to see Miss O'Connor other than in a manner that is required as part of your duties at this bank. Do I make myself clear?"

Mr. Harper regarded Schmidt sternly from across the desk. Schmidt felt himself redden, first in his face, and then the heat of the embarrassment crept down his entire body. "Yes sir, I am very sorry. I did not know . . . "

"Well now, Mr. Schmidt, you do. That will be all. Thank you." Harper turned to a shelf behind him and busied himself with some papers there. *The poor man*, thought Harper. *The poor man*. Schmidt left the office, and could not help but note the furtive stares and the quick turnings away of the other bank employees who had been watching through the glass. Claire was nowhere to be seen.

It was only after he was leaving the bank and had entered the pedestrian stream of Second Street that Schmidt saw Claire at last, waiting on the corner. She seemed to be watching the crowd, and he tried to catch her eye as he approached. As soon as he felt himself near enough to call out to her, however, she turned her gaze to someone else, a dashing young man who approached and caught her by surprise and prompted a peal of delightful giggling from her as he swept her up and they kissed. When they turned and joined the flow of traffic going off of Second, Hyrum Schmidt felt his heart hollow out and go cold.

The white edifice of the Pierce loomed ahead of him on the hill. The late autumn sunlight glinted off some of the Pierce's high windows and it almost looked like a place of promise. He thought to himself that he should like to go in there and stay for a good long time. Long enough that the world would forget him and he could ease himself out, board another train and be carried far away from here.

As he entered the Pierce that afternoon, he skipped the front desk where the boy, who had spotted him, waited to hand him what little mail he had. Schmidt continued across the lobby, into the elevator and up in to his room. He remained there for weeks. He ignored the urgent messages sent from Harper until they stopped altogether. He ate nothing. Eventually he heard about the stock market crash. From his window, he thought he could almost see a black pall descending over the city.

One day, more tired than he had ever been in his whole life, Schmidt embarked on the longest, most difficult journey he had ever taken. He rose from his bed and pulled a chair to the center of the room. Standing atop it, he took his necktie and secured it around his neck. *And they shall think, mein Gott, they shall think of me as having died for money. That is the saddest thing of all.* He fastened his necktie to the light fixture with one last act of artfulness, and then, before the urge of memory could claim any more of him, he kicked the chair out from under his feet.

POEMS

I.

Autobiography

A coverless book at the edge of the yard.

It must be winter and it must be at the margins

of what I know.

A biting wind turns the gray pages

without looking at them.

And of course, the wind cannot see,

at least not in this poem.

This book holds all of my rooms.

It holds those days that rose up

and pushed their obstinacy

like a cold car working along a path

plowed through deep snow.

I had my secrets; so did you.

Mom, there you are, staring

through me, out the window.

Dad, there's you, years later,

standing secretly outside

my closed bedroom door, straining

to hear the music I fed myself

when I thought I was alone.

A Cracked Storefront Window

The natural prayer of the soul: attentiveness.
                    Malebranche

I pass it for days,
this glass aware of its doom,
branched silver,

it is chance made beautiful,
a moment of contact, held
in the camera of the pane,

its frozen shatter
most plaintive and awake at night
when it pulses

with the luminous blood
of passing headlights:
Presence. Absence.

In the day
it's a ghost of itself,
a screen to veil

the wares sold there:
earth-colored pots, bowls,
candles fat with fuel

and little statues,
Buddha, silent
with his closed-eye smile
behind this curtain of accident.

Custodial

I used to mop the floors
in the detox ward, a line of doors
guarded by a coded lock
          that sundered
the patients' days from mine,
that portioned out their time,
as I wondered,

and soldiered against entropy,
what I'd do if it were me
and I had risen there,
          after wrong turns, blood burned,
and had to watch the world
from six stories up,
had to come clean, ride down, return.

The nuns who ran the place,
wore a hardened patience on their face,
and brooked no bullshit,
          for they'd heard
every last tale about falling down,
knew every promise was a gamble at best,
that half weren't as good as their word.

I must have changed
a thousand beds, arranged
pillows for as many heads,
          hauled legions of trash
in bundles down tunnels
to the ancient furnace,
all that trial and error turned to ash.

What was I doing there,
counting out my share
of wages, waiting between schools,
          my course uncertain?
The old priest—dubbed Father Mumbles—
blessed the patients daily, blessed me too,
his cassock, a hobbling black curtain,

he'd been at Bataan, a nurse said, sotto voce,
the death march had broken his body
into a crooked shadow, his wounds
        from a war I only knew as history,

but that I saw traced into
the offices of his prayer,
the limping shuffle of his ministry.

Sometimes, from a high window,
I'd watch an arriving ambulance below
pulsing red and golden
        as it came to us
from the city and its steady feed
of ruin, of pain, of plain bad luck, and anger,
of all that's ugly, but lit with something glorious.

Infusion

My life's paid out from a plastic box
and I walk differently under the sky

of boundless stars.
The lie of boundless stars.

I only have one planet and this is it,
the same one that breeds

panoplies in the biomes and in my blood.
I walk a shrinking circle drawn in chalk.

Chalk can drift into erasure, until there's only
the faintest ghost. So can a life.

My box whirs with each dosage it pumps
as its black numbers fold ever closer to zero,

and it hangs over my shoulder like a camera bag,
its clear tube and transport of silver fluid

easing into the disk nestled beneath the scar on my chest.
If you could take snapshots, little box, you'd see

gray auras hovering and hidden in the fanfare,
sodden pigeons picking for brilliance in the refuse,

a bulldog's grizzled gaze from a window, wet leaves
collaged on the infinity of dull pavement, each one

a fiery senescence,
a last page.

Wood

Split a piece of wood: I am there.
The Gospel of Thomas

                  My Dad
once showed me a plank that had just screamed out
from under a saw, pointed to how its waves, whorls,
strata, and trails of frozen current came to confluences
and could be seen as eyes in the grain, this man who
rarely let me glimpse the desperate quietude he carried,
curtained by cigarettes and beer.

                My Dad's Dad leans
into the old photo, blurred, the bare peak of the house
behind him, like that one in Wood's American Gothic,
only here, no wife, just a window, empty in the gray day
as he eyes the camera warily. *One mean son of a bitch,*
my uncle said decades after.

              My Dad sights a two-by-four,
a newly lit cigarette dangling from his mouth,
from which a bit of ash falls into a broken tumble
over the fresh wood.

Solemnity

I was glad the old song ended
and that we trailed out into silence.

It was August. Traffic whirred
obscenely beyond us

and the coffin slid so neatly
into its rack, the black door

shut so snugly, that I thought:
The world has become too practiced.

I wanted to leave that row of cars,
walk away alone across the asphalt,

over what was once our playground,
out to where it gave way to grass and

the route I used to take home, a path I'd mapped
behind those cheap apartments, the fence

with the hole in its mesh. Yes,
this is my prayer for now, and for always,

because the litanies and blessings have ended,
and I've chosen as holy, instead, that pause

after the leaves have whispered in their heights
and fallen silent, and I'm walking now

alongside the slumbering creek and winding road
to the hill that ascends to our street,

the row of houses that ends with ours, where out back,
the weathered fence still rattles between the yards.

Once, in another life, we had a world here
and watched the sky like an evolving mystery,

and even the small things were vast.
You were splayed on the grass,

no one, not them, not me, within sight,
only you alone and brilliant

arms spread under your firmament,
unmoored and adrift in your river,

mouthing those mute words
that are only yours.

Family Movies

i.
It was an old, old reel,
people as if painted, comical,
faces histrionic as clowns.
In the background, a beach
and the sea

the same old sea,
nothing fake about that, water
coming toward the patient camera,
a grainy play of white and black
always returning.

ii.
You used to call me away
from the edge of every lake
we drove to those summers.
I was a boy. The water was big,
a vault of memory in a slow gyre
sending opaque hands

to the rough dark shore and all
those sharp shards and hard stones.
When I turned in my nervous amble
back to your pale mask of worry,
I tried to beat the waves, each bare step
hitting broken shells and frigid rock.

All My Bright Little Beads

You keep coming back,
all you scattered phantoms

as fugitive as the divined paths
of assumed planets

or comets, those prodigal fuses,
so famous for their loyalty.

We say of shadows that they cast.
We say the same of spells.

I want to cast you off
and speed into new freedom.

Can I believe
that belief itself is enough

to scour your signature from me?
Can I hope that the hook at the end

of all my questions will claw me back
from the winter of your terminus?

You've taken enough days with your sear
and flare. I want to find a calculus

to return me to the time before you
began your burn.

When I was unscathed.
When I could bargain with my future

as if it were a field stretching green
in every direction, or water

fresh and running in the morning sun,
a rivulet tearing through the stasis

of what was the night's frozen pane.

Pluto

I remember that fifth-grade field trip,
the planetarium and the tiny old nun
who brought darkness, then lit the heavens up
to reveal the silver paths of the planets:

fleet, seared Mercury, our near neighbors,
Venus and Mars, and then Jupiter's fat globe
banded with roiling, million-year storms,
a world, she said, that takes twelve of our years

to lumber through its transit of our sun. I remember
almost floating out of myself as we traveled
to each celestial body and learned how they are named
for the ancient gods' iconic temperaments. I loved

the strange glory of Saturn, not gloomy at all,
so jeweled with its rings, and rainbow-striped
in every picture I'd ever seen of it. From there
we moved to the darker, colder outposts

and our questions about what might wait beyond.
I remember my walk home that autumn afternoon,
trees dropping their fire down to the streets,
lawns with the tentative assembly left by the wind.

I remember our house, quiet in those interim hours,
just my mother and me, and how I tried to tell her
what I'd learned of the planets, and how her eyes fell
on me briefly before her gaze veered off, fixed

upon the dark horizon of her past, a long-ago haunt
whose shadow I'd sometimes see cross over her.
I remember climbing to my room, thinking of all I'd seen
in that journey through planetarium darkness,

those far, cold, blurred worlds at the outer circles.
I remember how our house groaned in the wind
as I sat on my bed and I tried to picture ghostly Pluto,
a kingdom of silence, carrying its lonesome mystery.

House Fire, 1975

All the red screaming gets close and stops,
a black belching rises, two blocks over,
and I run, on fire myself with a frisson

to halt where soot climbs, shedding embers,
and bright curlicues of mesmeric orange
fever through every door and lintel.

Neighbors shamble over green lawns,
into an awkward gape
at this nightmare not theirs.

The woman crying through cat-eyed glasses
must be the one chosen by this blaze.
I watch her fall into a fold of arms,

a tide of consolation that drifts and encloses her,
men and women wading her way out of silence
from the crowd that can't stop watching.

The roof's been gashed with quick precision,
and a straddling fireman tosses down thick tears
of smoking black battens and sarking.

At the end of the hoses' arced torrents
a strange steady rain falls inside
all those rooms now seared free of memory,

nothing but charred lines and angles,
and I wonder what it will one day be for me
to walk into the black canvas of loss.

To Dream of Teeth

My mother and her mother
worshipped totems, prayer cards
showing martyrs' trademark wounds,
like St. Lucy, her plucked eyes
on a little plate, they could either be
a loss or one more look at a madly riven world.

Nights, I thought of those bodies
of the pious, torn, riven, and roasted,
asked God from the silence of my room
why he required trophies,
if he ever made them whole again,
or if they were lost to a madly riven world.

My mother told a Polish folktale:
to dream of teeth is to foretell death.
It seemed like a childish omen,
carried too long, a frayed telomere,
a dreaded light in an arena of fear,
a hedge against loss in a madly riven world.

The Demolition

Each day something new
tumbles out of it, a door
flung from a gone hall,
a nest of balding wire.

The torn syntax of pipes
bares its espionage to birds, wind,
as brick gives way to wood
and wood to space.

It is not nature, but seems so,
the way all the decades here
let loose in puffs of dust,
the way this long-buried litter
breaks free, splinters, errant cloth, debris
given the chance to fly from this.

At the corridor's broken terminus
each empty room rises up
to a new afterlife of sky

and I can't stop watching
as old space comes in to light.
It is what I want for myself,
this mystery of coming back to the world

like those old rooms with their new breath
suddenly rising in the wind of high corners
saying of their death
we never expected this.

The Hex Shank

Something minuscule has come asunder.
Void, that old insatiable giant, grows a little.
I have to walk down the hill because of a need.

What I want
is to draw back together what's been broken,
to let flow the curious water of repair.

I glow metastatic now. I'm a colander for light, blast me
with the rays of revelation and tell me what the shadows say,
the ones left behind, pulsing, rabid, and dirty.

Fuck them for staking a claim and refusing to go politely.
I told their kind as much after my father turned yellow
and shrank gradually into nothing but not before

he moaned from out of a morphine meander
and I spoke, trying to breach the thickness of his pain,
and knew he didn't hear his son, only swam

through a dim voice unmoored at the edge
of a floating luminous circle. But I prayed
to the window-shade of a God who plays

at coming out when no one else is looking. No one else
sees me now, and I don't believe The Man Upstairs
was ever really watching.

So I take myself to Handsome Juan, purveyor of hardware,
who's as dark, lit-up and world-weary as a Spanish saint,
who hears my complaint and summons the arcana

of tools, drill bits, and screws, which he pulls from an infinity
of drawers, cabinets of curiosities, elegance after elegance,
so tiny as to be invisible,

metal traces of threads whorled toward the vanishing point
on a tip that can bore into wood, innumerable pieces of steel.
I watch his hands and wonder if his blood is clean and free.

He does not know when he hands me my portion
how I note the blurred astronomy of moles along his forearm.
But he and I know the world goes wrong every day

in balances both known and unknown.
I pay and carry my wares out the door,
passing hinges, planed planks, pipes in myriad bends,

my body a harbor now for an off-kilter current,
the years behind me a road bordered by battered signs,
black arrows afloat in yellow fields, hinting a hazard.

Bitter Melon Soup

My Chinese mother-in-law
beckons us to suburbia
where we journey to receive

this thin yellowish-brew
that's steeped for days.
Good for cancer she tells me,

and then in Cantonese
to Jason, begins
to explain the process

of how to boil bones
and slice with precision
the oblong, warty melons,

to create the mix and
allow the proper time
for the blend to become

what it must. Forever *gweilo*,
I don't know the words
of her plosive language,

only that she's called upon
old and trusted powers
of harmony, and healing,

that her sons smile at
her faith in rote rhythms,
when on holidays she bids us

to place oranges at family graves,
light incense, bow three times
as she whispers to the departed.

I remember her silence
when we stood alone
a few minutes together

outside Bank of America
the day her husband died.
I tried to say with my eyes,

I'm sorry,
and hoped they said as well,
He was a good man.

Now I raise the soup to my lips
as Jason's brother watches,
amused, cringing to see my first sip.

He's tasted it before, shuns it,
but says, *More power to you.*
Yes, it's bitter, but rich too

like a breeze over a cemetery slope
bearing traces of wavering smoke
that rises from offerings for the dead.

Body Blow

I'm reading Whitman's *Specimen Days* as the city empties out all around me and Memorial Day looms, the big green book splayed open like a Bible on my kitchen island as I hover over it, and my archaic landline, suddenly alive in its cradle, jars me away from old white-beard and his fevered soldiers. I'm holding the phone in the main room, looking back now at Whitman left open in the kitchen, my doctor's voice on the other end, like it's farther away than this city—he says, *I don't have good news*—I think, *Not now* and remember that morning, how I'd had to lower my jeans under a blanket in the room kept cold for CT scans, *computerized tomography*, my body on the moving slab drawn slowly into the giant donut that powered up to an ominous hum and sent its light inside of my abdomen, searching for the source of the strange ache that had nudged me for weeks. He says, *I'm dancing around here, trying to avoid certain words . . .* And I start to fill in the blanks. *Just be straight with me*, I say. *I think it's cancer* is his answer. And I hear about the growths visible on the film he sees, one in my colon, more scattered across the lobes of my liver. I imagine them looking like showers and storm fronts on a Doppler radar. More words emerge: *prognosis, treatment, time.* He says, *I don't know enough. It's too soon.* I feel the days ahead as if they're gathering weight. *Is someone with you?*, he asks, and there will be soon enough, but when I hang up, I'm alone in a very new and sudden quietude. This is a holiday, everyone venturing away to enjoy the gift of one more day, one I'll have as well, and I think of a place, palm-lined, or at least warm, perhaps a beach, somewhere I'd rather be, where I can shed my clothes, take my body out into tropical light, to the edge of the water, into a breeze. I want it to carry me into forgetfulness. A decade ago, I posed nude for Bill, a painter friend, stepped out of jeans and t-shirt, taking direction to sit backwards on a chair, chin atop arms atop the curved crown of the chair's back, face hidden, light across my shoulders, thighs, arms, and my bowed head with its brown and precise brush cut. Months later I saw the finished canvas at a gallery on Union Square, and stood before it with a vague thrill of strangeness, seeing my pose, anonymous and faceless and yet me, just one of many men, each of us rendered like some spare Southwestern retablo of a saint. Bill had added, in a late flourish, a tattoo on my leg, an image of a carved log, a sprig of new leaf rising from it, something, shaman-like and resonant of blessing. I think of that portrait now, on someone's wall, or in storage among Bill's collected works, a separate body of mine, going its own way into a life I might have had. I imagine a time, in some bed in some room, when, like one of Whitman's young soldiers, caught within a failing body, I will look up and maybe see the old whitened father himself, the poet at my bedside, his face bright with the love of comrades. I would have no other God but this, forgive him for his duty of having to move from ward to ward, visiting upon me just a small interval, enough for a smile, a caress of his old hand upon my own thin and uncertain one, perhaps a brush of his capacious beard upon my yellowing face, his whisper, as soft as a breeze, just up against my ear, not a kiss, but a quiet and tender question: *Tell me your name, son.*

Absence

variation on a theme by Li Po

My father, visiting me,
stands on the slope of my garden
with its view of the west and the evening light,
his cigarette smoke snaking up
then lost in the late wind
coming down from Twin Peaks
where the fog begins its slow creep.

With the fog
all that rests above us begins to fade:
houses, perched and improbable
all along the hill. Facades, trees,
the road that leads down to us.
I watch the wind at play in his hair,
in the folds of his loose shirt, a current
that examines and then leaves him.
His cigarette burns to its end. We stand

watching the slow, far wavering
of things disappearing from the world.

II.

The Surrealist in Retirement

So you let your wide grin of clutter
gather here,
trumpets, bells, anima,
little pointed stars
of a universe.

You uncover
unfound houses
almost gone in
the great green paint
of thriving.

You tilt your face
up to the sun
and make another life
for yourself.

You will not pray,
you will not remember,
but there will be the night,
a jovial globe
behind your closed eyes.

Yellow, in Fourteen Chapters

i.

A stand in a faltering vicinity.

ii.

Somewhere between glory and vacancy.

iii.

I stitched myself somehow through brown days

toward you.

iv.

I didn't claw out a god or suffer for him.

v.

Some years were pocked and held on

but I out-walked them.

vi.

I didn't know about your beneficence

so far from the fence line, passing through

the gate of all those common trees.

vii.

Nothing dim wavered

or waited for my discovery, no

you were sudden—you always are—a floating amphibian

after days of littered jubilance.

viii.

I dream screens

as dark as slate, sand like water under their glass.

ix.

I suspect there is nothing more truthful than the weight

of a foot along a gravel path,

its punctuation keeping time.

x.

You are too common to be called deliverance.

xi.

I still remember how I once came into your clearing

as into an alien orbit.

xii.

No one else had the planet but me;

all my orchestras stopped.

xiii.

I saw the wind; I didn't hear it.

xiv.

I stood enveloped in your room,

changed by your multitude.

Penumbra

After The Rose, *by Jay DeFeo, painted over eight years (1958-1966)
and hidden behind a wall. The 2,000-pound canvas was discovered after her
death and removed by crane.*

i.

I will call this one red, a persistence.

I will build from maroon, mud, brown, burnt orange, umber.

All I know about it is that it is going to have a center.

I am a truant to this world.

I hold a mutable flower and feel off kilter.

In the beginning, void without form.

I will take this battered door and lean its bulk against the wall.

I will work when night's rain bends the light of the lonesome traffic.

Genesis. Kabbalah. The Guide for the Perplexed.

You had a tenancy with a long reign of obscure demands.

Down the long hallway, my sleep was a darkened wakefulness.

The sign atop the black sphinx down the street said: *Public Storage.*

And so we are hungry. And so we build by accretions.

It is true: I did not find your heart until much later.

ii.

A lifetime ago, I was new to this coast.

I painted a red claw across a map of the country:

where I'd been, and how I ended up here.

iii.

Time folds out from stars.

Year by year, I stumbled toward yours:

arms of your great radiance, order into entropy,

the long trip toward your anchorite bloom.

I carved your splayed light into sharp folds.

All your impasto wanted to fall from its splendor.

Rogue, you did not come easily out of my dark fabric.

Like a priestess, I ascended a ladder daily and reached up from risk.

All that I ached, contained you.

iv.

t is now the timeless later.

I'm long dead.

They had to break down walls to free you.

You breathed new air.

A fault ruptured.

Far away, I rested in the shadow of a mountain.

The Saint in Ecstasy

after Caravaggio

To swivel and fall
into this, the curved arm
of the street youth
modeling for the artist
as an angel

and the saint
just the shopkeeper
wrapped in the robe
of the Franciscan
for one day.

But the light finds them both:
the youth, bent, smiling,
the shopkeeper splayed, spent,
gone from the world,
his praise rising from its enclosure

and the boy cradling him
in his hunger.

The Cloud Brush

Japan's sumi-e painters
used a brush called
big cloud,

because it could hold
enough ink and water,
to rain down,

every shade from
the lightest gray
to the deepest black,

from a hazy blaze
of a white summer noon,
to a silvered snow bank,

from a steely loom
of storm-laden cold front,
to an obsidian midnight.

I picture it hanging,
its hewn handle
worn to a shine,

its generous wool
slate gray, dried,
asleep with its appetite,

and waiting
to be taken into hand again,
dipped expertly and then,

sending just enough
to make a mountain
to hold the trees,

to make a shoulder
of fog, like the shoulder
of a lover,

to make a moment,
a mood, a shadow,
all the tentative shelves

on which
the finer points of being
emerge by degrees.

It whispers
as it meets once more
the broad paper:

*I make this place
for a tendril, for a tern,
for a sleeve of fog*

*upon a stand of pines.
Here is a path
for a solitary walker,*

*I give you this,
one floating world
and then another.*

A Paul Klee Exhibit

Viewed in reverse chronological order

First his late trees:
blooms,
harlequin birds,

stems dissipating
into a purple cloud
or a head

all ballooned
on the strength
of having to be.

Not chaos, an array.
To become this
one has to unravel

from discernible life,
the fog and slow mania
permitted

from each suggestion
of structure—a body
reclining on a limb perhaps

or a landscape
etched in hairline strokes,
each blade of grass, each tree, each cloud

alive to dismantlement.
Quarks, they say,
quiver with a secret charge,

the smallest there is
and yet, they build us,
their leaps of faith

bringing us
to our fundamental element,
forever poised

between the luck of birth
and the brightness
of what's hidden.

Traffic Pylon on a Statue of David Hume

Edinburgh

A jolt of orange on a century of patina,
leaning now, this rakish crown
for Father Empiricist.

Someone
risked bruise and bone to posit this
Dada joke

and it's impossible not to look
at what the unheralded jester wrought,
and wonder how they must have leapt,

one vital living foot and then another,
laboring through a jump to dance upon
the philosopher's book of stone.

Shades

Inspired by the filming of Gus Van Sant's film Milk,
in San Francisco's Castro District, January, 2008

They brought back facades from thirty years ago:
the camera shop and Toad Hall. They parked old Chevys,
old VWs and old Fords, up and down the hill.
Each morning, each evening, I walked through the 1970s.

The past can be as present as a light you switch on,
or walk into. One night I watched Sean Penn climb atop a wall
to rally a crowd the way Harvey did. I stood in the chill
beside the machinery of illusion—a line of police dividing us.

This was a season of the walking dead, and I wondered
if any of those, gone now twenty years, might be there too,
staring out through bar glass and walking within
that remade river of candlelight. Or maybe only waiting,

like those men I passed every morning, each one
with a black jacket marked, SECURITY, each one
bored, lounging, and dozing beside the big white trucks,
guarding the apertures of memory.

A Fallen Bird's Nest

This bowl must have been hanging in its tree
above the cars and parking meters, above men
wrapped like pods and sleeping in doorways,
above the coffee cup lids, newsprint cubism, and
the quintillion cigarette remnants of sidewalk still life.

And now it's underfoot, a sudden flash on wet pavement,
its woven twig wreath, exploded out, but
still holding its circle, like some ring nebula
in a false-color photo of the stars.
This is not the universe as it is.

So here's an ignorance corrected into a kind of grief.
Its curve has spread, its center has opened
to cradle nothing, but two (or is it three?) ivory shells,
now shattered in the way all ruin is final and uncertain,
the yolks a perverse sun painted on the rained-on street.

And these men whose faces I never see sleep on as I pass,
and dream in ways the rest of us do,
of colors we forget could be the sun,
of the place beyond maps and cities, invisible lines,
where birds still follow their ancient path.

Hurricane

Anoles darted through the sunlight.
Up and down the streets, the peal
of ball-peen and apprehension.

Our days then were framed by the view
of what was encroaching upon us:
the maw of wind, clawfoot arms,
churning across latitudes.

Over uncertainty and distance
we prayed through the phone:
your voice, sometimes, came through weakly
but the code remained, riding the wave of words

that floated with its multitude, always above us.
When I finally got to you I saw the evidence:
lashed strands, tarp to thwart the wounded rooms
hanging empty over the gray beach.

On Bread and Pain

The storefront window script is French,
means *bread*, but I misread it first as English,

imagine a strange reverse commerce anchored
on this corner of shifting clouds and sun,

how each day, from houses along stolid streets,
the suffering would come to return it in bundles.

There'd be a lively trade in sorrow's blue-toned haunts,
and the body's maladies could supply a brisk business

in ache, jab, creak, burn, and thunder, every clutch
of these hurts weighed, appraised and left in wrapped packages,

done up and shelved in the white paper of forgetting.
But I think the most preciously tendered of all would be regret.

Each one of its stony hearts would echo with the footfalls
that brought its carrier to this door, where something very much like bread

would be handed across the worn wood in exchange, leavened
with absence, and tasting of dawn, a detour, an open road, and sky.

A Monk for the Rainy Season

Angkor Wat

The din of memory
falls again on the kapok trees
and the towered faces of the Bayon,
the green all around begins to erase
the paths to the temples.

He hangs up his robe of caked mud,
scroll of a lesser life,
and washes dried earth from his skin.

The sun slips
with this world's running dream
into the same sluice that goes down
in rivulets to sepulchral earth.

He draws a blade
over the crown of his head, cleans away
the dark cover of hair, washes clean
in the stream where everything
falls to the multitude of new rivers.

He takes the robe he's saved for now
and pulls it over arms that will stop their work,
over the body that will fold into the candle's flame

and open again within the gaze
of these gods who sleep, eyes closed,
smiling from one mute season to the next,
never ceasing to regard the world.

At Albion Street

i.
The steps up to your place
were blue hours in Tangier,
haunted Roman shadows,
a Paris hotel rank above
rue Gît-le-Coeur—
so many young men,
skin olive, gold, brown,
dragging with you
on white cigarettes
like a sacrament,
in Barcelona, Naples—
one more shaded room,
sleeping streets, a sultry stare
in an afternoon corner.

*Who is this American
who speaks the mother tongue
so well?*

ii.
Just near your door, one step
worn through, almost gone,
a broken Brooklyn, hanging,
like a page or a reverie
You'd warned me about it—
and each time I'd step over,
looking down into its eye.

Memory can swallow you up.

You meet me with your gaze
but your mouth wavers,
at play, undecided:

What language now,
to recite again
the beautiful words?

St. Huncke

Herbert Huncke (1915-1996)
Hustler, thief, writer

Christ was hung
between two thieves
and forgave them
amid the blaze
and fly buzz
of Golgotha.

Maybe he reckoned
that thievery is nothing
if not a borrowing of glory,
a barter no worse
than a small deception,
and worthy of mercy.

Once one could
steal a typewriter,
lug its heavy metal mouth
(archaic now in the way
all things will come to be),
its fount of creation,

and heft it just for cash.
How like a thief's boast,
a gallery of rogue stanzas,
that brash gamble,
to take on a burden
and be free of it in the same day,

the act of fencing,
a sacrament,

the act of borrowing,
a poetry all its own.

From Cole Street

At your front door all that week
new flowers, notes, a photo of you alone,
each morning I passed there I'd see
the tributes spread to you across the stone.

You were gone. It was quick. That is all.
And now these remnants at your closed door,
words written back to you, prayers that fall
beneath that placard in your window: No War.

Even late, you wrote a book to love,
to faces seen through café windows, doors down,
to newlyweds, young neighbors you lived above,
to Cupid and his career, and your own.

Once, not too far back, you led me up your stairs
so I could question you (while my tape recorder spun),
about your latest book, those poems to the affairs
of other poets, of other loves, of lives done.

Nice biceps, you said through an admiring smile
as I pulled you into the past from your front room,
and prodded you about metrics, subjects, style,
and tried to take notes, and left too soon.

On the street I held my recorder to my ear
to replay the tape on which our voices crossed,
but only a dead hum, no trace of us left to hear,
my questions muted, your voice, lost.

Thunderhead

The image on the screen is gray-green, mottled,
wind and rain abrading some street in the tropics.
The video stalls and buffers every few seconds
as if to make sure that this is indeed the world
and this reality is what must come down to us.

So we're that panic and shaky camera, and we watch
as it rises from the rain-lashed quotidian, through
a welter of slate-gray clouds and boundaries
running in the newly watercolor world. The ones
who live there can't believe it and we can't either,

the way this towered nimbus gleams with a luminous
iridescent crown, at first wobbling and then solid
within the frame, a rainbow inside of a humid bubble,
an anomaly beautiful but foreboding, under which
the locals cross themselves and seem to say a prayer

in the hope of preserving the world. We want to save it too,
and keep faith that the state of affairs will hold entropy
at bay. I remember how I stood, a child in my congregation,
fervent in the prayer that we raised toward the ceiling,
our hope going up to the waiting God we wanted,

world without end, Amen.

III.

Late Littoral

A gull's wings creak, whisper out of ashen silver
and lift from one state to another, over

this beach run ragged with seaweed, dull plastic and
all the detritus from the shrug of the water's currents.

The great bridge throws its red arm over the gate,
carries the ceaseless glinting traffic into midweek

and this gray lull of a day. I watch men venture naked,
each one's steps, and mine too, plowed into sand and

then eroded by stages as we head bridge-ward and back
over the browned, wet sand, its surface smoothed and

renewed in gentle pushes from the water's endless
breviary pages, each one a new arrival, then a retreat,

each one, erasing our insistent steps, water finding
and filling the little canyons we leave behind, all of it

timed, it seems, with the body and its ceaseless hungers.

Dolores Park

Glissades of men at basketball on the far courts
that blaze beyond your edge,

their shirtless clusters a mute and manic dance
I look to with unquestioned hunger

before turning back to your sloping lawns
that seem miles from the sclerotic traffic,

which is silent from my vantage and glinting
in its tired streaming around your boundaries.

You're named for the Mother of Sadness who waits
not far from here in verdant cemetery shadows

and leaning ruins. I am a body among bodies
in your territory, another dreamer come to doze

where old women shouldering bulbous garbage bags,
harvest overflowing bins for beer-fumed glass and plastic,

and certain men in sunglasses work a surreptitious circuit
to peddle weed with troubadour mumbles.

Oh how this heat and cannabis lilt
settles upon us, so like the wash of Lethe,

and summer music wavers, tentative
from a thousand little boxes under the vault

of this cloudless interval over us.
A droning cruciform plane passes in transit and fades

and this great blue that burns overhead
is just a leaven, a curtain of mimicry as false

as the promise of our own skin, which lets us
call ourselves whole even though we're permeable,

and tethered to a sparking, spooky circle
as much as any atom, as much as any star.

Vanishing Point

My friend Robert vanished.
"I might just disappear," he said

over the phone months before,
holding the prospect of it out

like a hoop to be jumped through.
He needed me to receive

his folded prophecy,
to read the hermetic economy of

his random dispatches, like the text
about a bookstore he thought I'd like,

and I did. But he wasn't there,
or anywhere else, his name gone

from its rectangle by the button
that I still pressed from the lobby

of his building. That bookstore
is gone now too, in its space,

of all things, a gym with a boxing ring
where for a price and a limited time,

two can dance,
each one circling the other

in feint and spar,
each one trying to guess

the next move.

Five Sapphics for Three Young Men

getting into a big car. Two back, one front.
Bodies fluid on a hinge like a screen door.
Bodies in the summer breeze, errant, sexy,
Hawaiian, one seems.

I've been walking, heavy with an old desire.
I'm old enough, I carry love and doses.
Take me with you, today is sunny, fervent,
I could ride shotgun.

It looks like lunch brought you out, I see the bags,
sodas in hand, where to go from here? This is Friday,
maybe we could drive beyond the day, skip work,
shed our clothes beachside.

But you're gone now; the street yawns under the sun.
Bodies have a law their own. I turn, walk on.
Maybe it was chemical, the way I gazed,
wanted you, transfixed.

I slog uphill, homeward bound, the fog far out
begins to reach the spindly signal tower
above Twin Peaks. I always prefer the dream.
My cat waits, sleeping.

Aubade, Serenade

after Ovid

I wake up
to the peal of riven wood,
nails, saws and men
at work on the rising frame
of a house next door.

It sat silent the night before,
halted in its shape,
just as darkness began its creep,
lights coming on up and down the street,

and mine out, as you'd agreed we'd meet:
no light, no words, no sleep, just you
stepping, white limbed, out of jeans,
and me, transformed too,

only the moon's spilled glow
on the ground around our naked feet.

A Brief History of My Lust, His Visitations

The first time, a fresco's blossom
fresh in famished paint.

Thereafter, a pair of dark eyes,
like some saint staring through ordained fire.

Always, my blood in a manic pulse.
Sometimes, a gold incandescence in the dusk,

a garden shed, a pulled-down shade.
There's a mute warble, the late sun

orange and wobbly
over some back wooden stairs.

It's tantamount to surrender—this ascent
again within view of the ocean at the edge

of our city. Dalliance. Entrechat. And even now
waves still twinkling in the window's slate gut.

Call it a multitude, the sure moon
on an infinity of empty dinner plates.

Walk the water's edge.
There's hunger in its pinioned turbulence,

another surge, and crest, and plaintive hush
of false resolution, rolling forward

again and again and again.

Moby

Later he told me the mythology of his car,

the big white one he got from his dad

who smoked and drank a lot and owned

a bar called The Pagoda, a bit of Asian kitsch

tucked behind a sunbaked strip mall, where

he'd washed glasses as a kid, and where on slow days

his dad would sometimes pour a line of vodka along the bar

and light it, just so they could watch a second or two

of pure fire before his dad wiped it away with a cloth.

Even a flame can vanish before leaving its mark

if you erase it fast enough. And so he got the Mercury,

whose roof leaked so much he had to stuff in towels,

and sometimes diapers, to stop the rain. It creaked too,

was as battered as the fabled whale he named it for.

I met him online—fantasy matched for fantasy,

and when I saw him for the first time, walking to me

down the hill from where he parked his storied wreck,

I stood in my gate thinking *he's too young*, but I stayed.

I must have known his current was the same as mine, each of us

from flat towns where you could always see the horizon, each of us

veterans of quiet upstairs rooms and secret song-filled hours

where we waited above the undertow of our parents' solitudes.

The Known World

A cold wind comes to claw the cottage,
knocks limbs against roof, wall, window,
each tree an alien of restless arms,

as we tangle, body to body,
in the cluttered darkness of our one room,
and the evening sputters just beyond us,

as if sending us its agreement with
our hungry grasp and climb upon each other,
our heat turning to water upon the windows.

Somehow, we ease into a lull, this engine
evening out into rest, as a simpler hunger
overtakes us, and we dress, walk into the cold,

down the hill from our aerie to the avenue
that proclaims, in illuminations, the food on offer:
Italian, Mexican, Peruvian . . . we pass

into the warmth of a Korean place,
huddle over bowls of broth with fish so small
their bodies look like silver hyphens,

each of us cradling a little sea of them,
filling ourselves with what were once
whole currents of eyes in a shimmering school.

We've come here from a world away,
our secret quarter still waiting in the night above,
and take this necessary communion,

while outside, lights of shop windows, of neon,
of traffic eliding in its river, all glow in fog's halo,
certainty and doubt, in their endless wavering.

Fortune Cookies

After the meal we crack these brown shells
and tug thin paper from their dried mouths,
strings of lucky numbers and words that you glance at
then ignore. You don't know this
but when they bode well for us I save them, secretly
pluck their promise from the refuse of our table
to file them in my wallet, where they collect
mingling, brushed against the currency we spend.

The Spite House

We walk amid unattainable mansions
and money's wake in the streets, gold leaf
adorning shop windows, all this new heritage

of the waxed handlebar, reclaimed wood,
and glasses of craft. They sell it with poetry,
those menus of the arcane, and we've ventured

to taste of some of it. But most evenings
we cultivate a middling scorn
for every antlered living room, golden light

spilling from certain windows. Through others,
a bookish mess that's real, or out front, steps
rising humbly from truant gardens to a solid door

closed tight. Once, I pointed at a sliver
of a house, wedged where no house should be,
surmised its façade to be Federal, guessed

its builder had long ago staked a bitter claim
because he could, and paid incredulous carpenters
to raise this improbable home borne of argument.

We figure it's all ancient history, smile
at that other old saw: history repeats.
You say, *I like the way the red door pops.*

Ellipse

My first neighborhood,
        my solar system.

I enter its far edge with you,
        show you the market, now abandoned,

the drugstore, defunct too,
        these, the outer belt's dead ice.

Houses flake into pale acedia.
        March relentlessly delays spring.

All along these lanes I revert
        to memories you never knew.

We cross ancient orbits:
        the Jupiter circuit where

I once circled in glee
        on hand-me-down bikes,

the martial boundaries where
        I battled over yards' territories.

And then the center, my old house,
        now foreign, empty.

A brown vine rattles up brick
        beside the porch, something

we would have cleared
          long before it could climb.

I see my two brothers, myself, again,
        we three, directed

to pluck Autumn's fallen flames
        off of our lawn,

my mother upstairs . . .
        . . . my father down,

each of them
        at their own window.

Walking through this late winter,
          you stop me, point up

to a cardinal—as bright as fire—
              singing from a bare branch.

I've brought you here as my witness,
but now you show me the world.

Book of Hours

Green-sage feline eyes that I always see as human.

He usually sleeps between us, the warm engine of
his breathing a temblor and pulse from within
his furred bulk, a density I feel against my own.

Mornings when I wake, he stirs in concert with me.
He's been waiting, knows my rhythms as I know his,
knows too how we found him, carried him home and

hold him now within the circuit of our sure habits.
When we kiss and entangle and answer to our urge,
he pulls back to his mysterious station, his own time,

and waits with quietude for our animal fervor to feed
toward its resolution. And if I look up from our quickened
breaths, and if he chances to look back, it is with a gaze

that is solemn, wise, patient and ancient.

Love

Love lives at the corner
of Prince Street and Broadway
amid dishrag air and the shrill of renovation
where the beverage cart man
pushes annoyance across the heat
and a father leans toward his boy
in a shadowed doorway.

I carry a copy, just bought,
of Islamic mystical poetry,
entreaties to a God impatient,
a God unseen, a stolid God who sits
as each new day sends up its tendrils
of prayer.

Down here in the throng
youth blazes towards us
and I tell you it's okay as it passes
incarnate along these brown boards
that skirt gaping holes of excavation
where sun sears old pipes and the scurry
of displaced rats, and we know we're as old
as we've ever been.

I'll take this year and its tentativeness.

I'll read Rumi in the clouds
as we fly out from this city
into the all-too-shallow pool
of blue and pollution
far above the absent towers
and new ones trying for heaven.

Love is our arc across the continent
over states we imagine empty.
Love is all the furrowed rows of seed.
Love is each little pearled light
nudging across the crooked, worried quilt
that is the land's darkness.

Big Sur

I'm nervous on this road,
carved like a shelf into the
high cliffs that skirt
the Pacific.

I drive and you gaze
at the ocean below us,
its slow churn almost lost
along its infinite slate table, and

at each curve, I ease our speed,
grateful when the pines
intercede between us
and the depths below.

The next day, safely in place,
we venture through woods
and into a morning clearing where
milky mist waits on green slopes,

before we pass into trees again.
Our days are slow here, the breath
of our walking new to us. Rain
visits like a steady blessing.

The largest powers
carry their essence invisibly,
like the far violence of stars.
We cut our path beneath them.

Days later, driving back,
I hug the road again but sneak
a look at the unceasing ocean,
catch sight of a great wave

breaking into spray over a rock
far out from our promontory.
We had to leave the familiar
and come to the boundaries

of this hard and crumbling shore,
see the pleading of wave against
ancient strata, its persistence
like the tendered negotiations of love.

Lifeline

Nothing reached me except
a death sentence and doubt.

I knew that black cables
pulsed on the bottom of the ocean

crossing the great darkness
between the continents

with voices other than mine,
a multitude of ambition and hunger.

I crumbled against a wall of transit
and cried

amid all that thundering on
toward silence.

And then the tunnel
opened into a muted daylight,

peaked rooftops under
a sky of pewter ribbons and rain.

My dead mother and father
surfaced in memory, each one

looking down with me
at the tableaux of their last beds

and last days. Their faces said:
It won't be the same for you.

On my way home, I passed torn-open
garbage bags, sidewalks of flotsam.

We make such bright things
and hope.

Spills of green glass,
recent plunders, crunched underfoot.

I stood at the bleak intersection,
the bottom of the hill that looked up

to the sky's emerging canvas of blue
where a white moon hung, traced there

almost like a whisper:
There are other worlds than this.

AFTERWORD

"Our World"—it was a term Jim and I used to describe the characters and personalities we superimposed onto our everyday lives. In our funny cartoon world, mailboxes thanked us in chirpy, high-pitched voices when we sent letters; our bright green car smiled and greeted us each time we took a ride. Jim kept record of our world in both his journals and the little scrap-paper notes he left for me all around our home. I will always treasure one note drawn on the back of an envelope while I was home sick one day. He had written the line "Monsters caring for each other" at the bottom because that's what we were—two little boy monsters who loved each other so much and held each other tight during storms and scary times.

When Jim died from cancer in 2018, our world of fifteen years shrank to almost nothing for me. Everyday life devolved into a soup-like fog of grief and I didn't want to get out of bed most days, but I still managed to keep a routine. Sorting through Jim's papers and emails each day helped me—keeping his work alive was a way to keep myself alive too. I continued to sign off on releases for some of his poems and monitored the progress on outstanding manuscript submissions he had sent off before he entered hospice. I also submitted Jim's work to the literary and poetry competitions that kept popping up in his inbox, because after reading his final journal entries, I better understood the heightened emotions and desperation he experienced wanting to be remembered in print— something he was never able to talk about while he was alive. I knew I had to keep submitting Jim's work for the sake of our world, where all the talking mailboxes, cars, and animals were still encouraging me.

After reading about Leland Cheuk's journey and founding of 7.13 Books, I sent him a heartfelt letter comparing his illness and challenges with Jim's, but with one major exception: Jim didn't live through his illness and get to have his first book published. I went on to describe Jim in more detail, in part to drive home the tragedy of losing such a good writer. As I wrote Leland:

> *It's become a mission for me to finish this for him and help*
> *fulfill his dream. By keeping his work alive, I'm able to hold*
> *onto something more than personal photographs and memories.*
> *By sharing his work with a larger audience, I'm able to keep a*
> *part of Jim alive.*

Who wouldn't do something like that for someone they loved?

When Leland wrote back to say he wanted to take a chance on Jim's work, the entire anthropomorphized neighborhood cheered for us, but all I could do was cry because Jim couldn't celebrate with me. I wish it hadn't taken Jim's illness and death to get him noticed.

After three years and a global pandemic, I still talk to Jim every evening as the sun sets. As I close the blinds and turn on the lamps, I tell him how the day went and that I wish he were still here with me. I can see his responses through little signs in the world—a cat darting out from under a car, a favorite song that suddenly comes on the radio, or a certain feeling in the air as the seasons change. I often hear his voice describing something or recounting a funny story. Jim's voice is out there in the rest of the world now, thanks to this book. I hope you can hear him, too.

This book wouldn't be possible without Leland Cheuk and our poetry editor, K.B. Thors. Special thanks to Margaret Stowawy and Michael Walsh for their unending encouragement and support, Richard Schneider and the *Gay & Lesbian Review* who gave Jim an outlet and showcase for so many years, Rachel and Shana for their blessings, Michael Carroll for his love and for helping me see a broader picture of Jim through his past, and Edmund White for his sensitive, thoughtful insights. We did this together, all for Jim. *Monsters caring for each other.*

—Jason W. Wong

ACKNOWLEDGMENTS

America Magazine, "A Fallen Bird's Nest"

Arroyo Literary Review, "The Cloud Brush," "Vanishing Point," and "Pluto"

A&U Magazine, "Shades." This poem also appeared in the magazine's anthology, *Art & Understanding: Literature from the First Twenty Years of A&U* (2014)

Chelsea Station, "Body Blow"

Chroma Journal, "Hurricane"

Collective Fallout: "The Ballad of Tangleton"

Connecticut River Review, "Custodial"

Fourth River, "The Known World"

Gay & Lesbian Review Worldwide, "From Cole Street." This poem also appeared in the anthology, *The Place That Inhabits Us: Poems from the San Francisco Bay Watershed* (Sixteen Rivers Press, 2010).

IDK Magazine, "The Hex Shank" and "Moby"

Kyoto Journal, "A Monk for the Rainy Season" and "Absence"

Mudfish, "The Surrealist in Retirement"

Nimrod, "Bitter Melon Soup" and "Five Sapphics for Three Young Men"

Poetry: "A Cracked Storefront Window" and "A Paul Klee Exhibit"

Sacramento News and Review, "Fortune Cookies"

Santa Fe Literary Review, "Ellipse" and "A Brief History of My Lust"

Slur: "A Wasp Nest"

St. Sebastian Review: "The Saint in Ecstasy"

The New Engagement: "Love," "Lifeline," and "Autobiography"

Third Wednesday: "Traffic Pylon on Statue of David Hume"

"Aubade, Serenade" appeared in an earlier version in the journal *Yuan Yang.*

"At Albion Street" appeared in the privately printed memorial anthology, *The End is the Beginning—Elegy for a Carnivorous Saint: A Memorial Collection for Harold Norse* (2010).

"St. Huncke" appeared in an earlier version in *Empty Mirror.*

"The Demolition," received an Honorable Mention in *Glimmer Train*'s Poetry Open competition and was published on the journal's website.

"A Paul Klee Exhibit" was also featured as the "Poem of the Day" on the website *Poetry Daily.*

ABOUT THE AUTHOR

Jim Nawrocki's work has appeared in *Poetry*, *Kyoto Journal*, *Nimrod*, *Arroyo Literary Review*, *The Gay & Lesbian Review Worldwide*, *Chelsea Station*, *poetrydaily.com*, as well as many other journals. It has also been anthologized in *The Place That Inhabits Us: Poems of the San Francisco Bay Watershed* (Sixteen Rivers Press, 2010) and *Art & Understanding: Literature from the First Twenty Years of A&U* (Black Lawrence Press, 2014). The poems in this book, collected under the title *House Fire*, won the 2009 James White Poetry Prize, judged by Mark Doty. He passed away from cancer in 2018.